Kipligat's Chance

David N. Odhiambo

PENGUIN
CANADA

PENGUIN CANADA

Published by the Penguin Group

Penguin Books, a division of Pearson Canada, 10 Alcorn Avenue, Toronto, Ontario,
Canada M4V 3B2

Penguin Books Ltd, 80 Strand, London WC2R 0RL, England

Penguin Putnam Inc., 375 Hudson Street, New York, New York 10014, U.S.A.

Penguin Books Australia Ltd, 250 Camberwell Road, Camberwell, Victoria 3124, Australia

Penguin Books India (P) Ltd, 11, Community Centre, Panchsheel Park,
New Delhi – 110 017, India

Penguin Books (NZ) Ltd, cnr Rosedale and Airborne Roads, Albany, Auckland 1310,
New Zealand

Penguin Books (South Africa) (Pty) Ltd, 24 Sturdee Avenue, Rosebank 2196, South Africa

Penguin Books Ltd, Registered Offices: 80 Strand, London WC2R 0RL, England

First published 2003

1 3 5 7 9 10 8 6 4 2

*Publisher's note: This book is a work of fiction. Names, characters, places and incidents either
are the product of the author's imagination or are used fictitiously, and any resemblance to
actual persons living or dead, events, or locales is entirely coincidental.*

Manufactured in Canada.

NATIONAL LIBRARY OF CANADA CATALOGUING IN PUBLICATION DATA

Odhiambo, David Nandi, 1965–
Kipligat's chance / David N. Odhiambo.

ISBN 0-14-301233-9

I. Title.

PS8579.D54K56 2003   C813'.54   C2002-904654-8
PR9199.3.O318K56 2003

Visit Penguin Books' website at **www.penguin.ca**

For my beloved wife, Seonagh
Mum, Dad, Lydia, Sophie, Debra, Joe, Michael and David Jr.
—who are all my touchstone and my meaning.

Kipligat's Chance

Prologue

At sunrise, between the cock's first and second crows, Koech high steps to the distant rumble of a train. His breath ivory in a landscape clipped by a guinea fowl's clapped wings, his bigass afro tipping grandly in the wind.

He shambles into a clearing and descends towards a clear stream, perch swimming in clusters through its shallow bed. Then he disappears into a swivel of sugarcane before reappearing with dew-clad ankles among grazing grounds once populated by the sausage tree.

I crouch behind a thorn bush and watch him spit phlegm gathered like snuff between his gums. Thin lizards scatter as his feet crush beetles feeding on dung. Alone. Bulling forward, like the warthog from salt lick to waterhole.

He runs through tufts of dry elephant grass, nameless hills and into spirals of red dust, then gathers himself before a gouge in the trail. He lunges, hangs from weeding time till the second crop before emerging tall, taut, his belly a grumbling gourd.

Bells clang where young boys tap sticks against the flanks of cattle. Sweat brands his forehead. Koech, the one born with an *umbilical cord wrapped around his neck, finds his mark in the soft underbelly of the land of the crocodile.*

He holds his shoulders high. Fragile. Cloistered. His slack face teased by the eye of the sun. Past the telephone line, in silence.

As soon as he's within ten feet, I stride forward onto the path and run as if I too wear a headdress plumed with ostrich feathers. He laughs, closing on me fast. Roasted groundnuts toss about in my pockets as I run out ahead for the first time since the new moon began to pick up the flight of small insects.

1

SEPTEMBER:
The Game

There are two great tragedies in life. One is not to get your heart's desire. The other is to get it.

—GEORGE BERNARD SHAW

1

It's a choice September morning; Kulvinder and I prance about in T-shirts and shorts at the start line of the Richmond Five-Mile X-Country Challenge for Juniors. We're chronic with jitters, two mates in our first race in four years. Out to prove that ain't nobody got game the way we do.

Behind a nylon rope, former Olympian Sam Holt paces with a stopwatch hung around his neck. He's the mack with the flavour. The hooked-up Don looking for the ones worth uploading onto his revamped Achilles Track Club.

He's decked out in a shrunken red tracksuit, the top barely containing his belly, his sweats too tight at the balls. Not that he gives a fig, his only care being the roster of split times scrolling through his noggin.

Kulvinder and I are quite possibly the youngest runners in the race. Sixteen going on seventeen while the others are older, hairy-legged, hairy-knuckled buggers.

I look his way, hoping to get his attention. But he's strapped to a Walkman and psychs himself up to any number of M.C. Hammer's pre-gangsta rap joints.

Kulvinder's the Punjabi equivalent of Shaft. Hard-muscled. Features drawn with a geometry set. His nose is an isosceles triangle, his mouth a trapezoid. Even his shaved head an ellipse on which a discarded white turban used to sit. In comparison, my waist, around which Koech's blue sweat top is wrapped by its sleeves, drops to a pair of nubs for knees. All I'm missing is tortoiseshell spectacles held together with black electronic tape.

I tap him on the shoulder. "I've changed my mind," I say. "I don't think it's such a good idea to run with the lead pack."

Ice blings at his neck. "You know we've got to stay with those two-bit yobs if we're going to impress Sam."

"I'm running in the field." I never should have let Kulvinder talk me into this in the first place. Koech is the talented one in my family.

"Suit yourself, mate." He places the headphones back on his ears.

I circle the infield like a clod with a finger up my sphincter, searching through a busload of supporters from school for a glimpse of Stephanie "Jugs" Bates.

She kicks it with a group of girls ankle-deep in yellow maple leaves. Sun pouncing all up in natural blonde hair, matty not curled. Her Fubu sweats and purple nail polish match her thickly smeared lips.

Two hours after her folks moved into the suite upstairs from mine last month, she knocked on our door.

"Help." A black push-up bra peeped over the top of her blouse's plummeting neckline. "91.6 FM is giving away two free Funky Live Jamboree tickets to their ninety-first caller.

Five bands have been announced, but their special guest ain't confirmed. Nuff said. Mum wants me to roll on over to the convenience store 'n pick her up feminine product. Tampons 'n shit. I get ten percent off, y'know, employee discount 'n all. Could you dial the digits for me while I'm gone?"

We haven't talked much since then. But that's about to change. If I run well, it'll be obvious I'm the stallion to be taken out to stud.

"We go in thirty seconds," shouts the starter into an intercom.

I'm scared dickless, no bones about it. Some of these squits have calf muscles the size of grapefruit. Others are sponsored and wear ritzy kits stitched together by kids in Taiwanese sweat shops.

It's intimidating as all hell. So much so that my hands shake when I untie the top from around my waist. Digging a thumb in. Trying to get the damn knot loose. Dang. I crouch, bend forward, stretch the sleeves up to my mouth and use my teeth. The arms loosen, slip, the top dropping turd-like behind me. All while the sponsored nimrods execute a series of skillfully executed leaps.

"Runners take your marks," yells the starter.

Dutifully I trot out among this sorry collection of eighteen-year-old wankers.

BANG.

A surge of bodies knocks me to the ground, and I grasp a pair of shorts, red Lycra ripping in my hand. By the time I return it to the owner and clamber back to my feet, the pack is forty metres on.

I tear after them. Head up, feet scuttling through mud, chest out until five minutes later I slip into the back of the lead pack.

The pace is quick, and I hang on as we plod through trails of muck.

It's a relief when the route narrows. Forcing us to slow down and run in single file through dense pine and cedar. We slog through puddles of mud, duck under brambles and stutter-step over braids of twisted tree roots, a group of about twelve of us spilling out onto an open field three-quarters of the way around the first loop.

It's the first real chance I have to catch my breath. But Kulvinder's stride lengthens, and he pumps his arms like he's hot-wired on caffeine.

I hate it when he goes off like that.

A small group of us follow the potty-tosser into a series of rolling hills, the wind gusting into our faces in waves, each blast damn near knocking us off our feet.

He varies the pace, pushing up a long hill before backing off for a couple of short ones, then cranking it up for two more long ones before slowing down again.

It's raining, and my thighs ache like they've clubbed and ground all night, bumping to Isaac Hayes.

By the time we finish the first loop, a stitch above my right hip hurts something fierce.

To my left Sam leans over the rope with his stopwatch, and I put in a half-assed spurt. The others breaking away, their arms and legs working with an intensity I can't match.

I key on the figure ahead of me. "Keep your feet moving. One more loop to go." Pushing and pressing along the muddy trail until I'm back in the open field. "Keep working." I bend into the gut-busting wind and chase him up a hill. "Two hills hard. One easy." Cows graze behind a barbed wire fence.

"Three hard. One easy." Jamming it in his mug with a little less than half a lap to go. "Three hard. One easy."

I close in on a cluster of runners. "Two hard. One easy . . ."

When I cross the finish line, I collapse.

Kulvinder's waiting there to help me to my feet. "Good show." Huge flakes of dirt are splattered all over his face; everything beneath his knees is caked in mud. "But you've got to keep moving."

He loops an arm around my waist; I shiver and lean into his shoulder.

"How . . . did . . . you . . . do?" I pant.

"Not bad." He hands me a water bottle. "Drink. You need liquids."

"What's . . . not bad?" I take the bottle from him.

"Second."

"That's . . . great . . . dog."

"It's not bad." He takes the flannel blanket he's been wrapped up in and throws it over my shoulders.

We bundle up and I tremble against him as we warm up on a grassy mound near the finish.

I'm happy he's being nice to me. He could be rubbing my face in how serious I got smoked. Easy.

Kulvinder's eventually called away for the award ceremony, and I see him gab with Coach Holt. The former Olympian hikes up his sweat pants, accentuating the rotundness of his boys.

On Kulvinder's way back Jugs stops him.

Whoa!

His hands touch her arm, and they laugh before she flicks dirt from his brow.

He breaks it down on his return. "You got eighth place," he says. "They've got all the results on a sheet of paper near the finish."

I'm stoked. But I also feel a little shy. So I change the subject. "What did Sam say?"

"He said he liked what he saw and wants me to train for the 800 with his track club."

"What about me?"

"Didn't I tell you to run with the leaders, mate?"

"I tumbled at the start."

"He doesn't think you have the endurance."

"But I fell."

"No worries. I'll talk to him."

I look down at the ground.

Kulvinder punches me hard in the triceps. Twice. Then snatches the blanket from my shoulders. "I said I'd talk to him."

My fingers tingle with pain, and my upper arm is numb.

"Listen, I'm going to the dance with Jugs tonight. I hope you don't mind?"

"Mind! Don't be daft." I've never told him how much I like her. Not really. I'd only joked about the buxomness of her titties. "I don't have dibs on her."

"You certain?"

"No doubt."

He wallops me harder than the time before. "Chin up. She's bringing a friend she says is off the charts."

"Not interested."

I pull on the drawstring of Koech's sweat top and hide in the hood. If he hits me again, I'll blub my eyes out.

"Chin up," he says. "I said I'd talk to Sam, all right?"

He should probably whack me a couple more times for good measure. It's what I deserve.

What kind of idiot gets excited about eighth place? Sam didn't. Jugs hadn't. Koech wouldn't. He'd be cursing and kicking the bark off a five-hundred-year-old Douglas fir.

After the cross-country race Kulvinder and I career west on Broadway in Mrs. Sharma's Chevy, then turn south onto Main Street. He's moved beyond the race and prattles on about his date with Jugs, looking at me instead of watching the road.

"Do you think you could keep your eyes on what you're doing?" I suggest.

He parps his horn, runs the table of amber lights, and speeds towards Second Avenue.

I change the subject. "Did Coach Holt really say I have no endurance?"

Kulvinder pushes Afrika Bambataa into the tape deck and pumps up the volume.

"Just give us the bottle of Southern Comfort in the glove compartment."

I present him with the booze and get quiet.

"You going to have a taste?" he asks.

"Not till later."

"Not till later," he mimics in a falsetto whine.

"I can't afford to go home reeking of alcohol."

He lifts both hands off the steering wheel and accelerates through a red light.

"Kulvinderrr."

He laughs before braking behind a van illegally parked in the middle of the street. A strapping bloke in a green uniform unloads a computer from the vehicle's boot.

Kulvinder parps his horn again.

"I think he left a couple of inches there I can still squeeze through."

He rolls down his window.

"Take your time, mate," he says. "Never mind us."

"I'll be out of your way in a second, sir."

Kulvinder rolls up the window. "Fabulous!"

He chugs down more booze, then shivers.

"Let's get a pint at Billy's Tavern," he says. "I don't feel much like going home."

"Nah," I reply. "I told the folks I'd be back by four."

"Gawd, you can be a bore." Kulvinder looks in the rear view mirror, backs up real quick and squeals onto a side street.

My feet peddle hard against the floor mat as I instinctively search for a brake.

He swerves up onto the sidewalk and knocks over a garbage can.

I clutch the dashboard. "Stop the car!" He drives through a flower bed, flips a finger out his window at a startled old couple on their porch, then turns back to the road.

"Like I said, boooooring."

With one hand I take the bottle from him, and with the other I grip the door handle.

3

It's after nine when I get home. Not a good move since I said I'd be back that afternoon. But I couldn't even think of returning till we'd sobered up a little. Now I'm in for a beef with the folks.

No matter. I've got a more pressing concern: the thought of Kulvinder at the dance with Jugs has me bugged. It can't happen. Screw the consequences. I'm going to stop by her crib and lay my feelings on the line.

I walk down our block in the East End and through a corridor of strung-out tarts wearing tight rayon hot pants.

"Hey, Chan Lu."

"Whats'up, Leeds."

"Raquel."

"Sweetie."

I'm on a first-name basis with most of them. Not because of steamy encounters in the alley out back. No, no, no. They're not the type I go for. It'd be downright depressing to smoke one of those cellulite-laden asses. All humping tainted by the thought of their attention deficit spawn, crunching away at a diet of Captain Crunch cereal in a rinky-dink hovel.

"Another slow night?" I ask.

"Not for that whore, Yvonne." Chan Lu replies. "Braggin on my ass about all the dick she scored."

"It'll pick up."

She adjusts her skirt. "Got any money for cigarettes, honey?"

"Everything comes at a cost," I joke.

She blows me a kiss. "Wait till I tell your mum what a dirty mind you got."

I push on a latch, lift up the gate and shove.

Our two-storey house isn't much to look at. The white paint is peeling; cracked windows are held together by duct tape. The yard of overgrown grass is sprinkled with rusty automotive parts, and the wire fence surrounding it all is overrun with morning glories.

What gets me the most is that the light on the porch is toast, a constant reminder that Mr. Chen is a slumlord.

I stand in front of Jugs' door, a finger on her doorbell. My armpits sweat and my jaw is clenched. The chain-link fence hiccups trapped refuse into a gust of wind.

WHRRRRRPBUP.

The door bangs open and Slim, her eight-year-old brother, scampers out.

"Whoa." I catch him by the arms to avoid a collision.

His pasty face is smeared with dirt, and the brown hair on top of his head is like new growth in a clear-cut.

"Slow down there, dog."

He's out of breath, "ZZzzup?"

"Where you off to this time of night?"

"See the bitch."

"Who?"

"My girl."

"Oh. Is Steph around?"

"Nah, she atta friend's."

"Damn." I missed her. "Well, be sure not to stay out too late."

"Whatever," he snickers before barrelling off into the night.

After overhearing the bungling on the porch, Mum opens up.

She's wrapped in a kanga, a dab of toothpaste sitting over her upper lip.

"Where in heavens name have you been?" She sounds relieved.

"Kulvinder had a flat tire." I've bombarded my mouth with garlic. "We got stranded out in the sticks without a spare. Thank God, a rock band pulled over and gave us theirs." I cross myself and look at the ceiling. "Thank God."

"You're drunk." She's furious.

Dad calls her name from the living room, sneezes, then bellows for the hot water bottle.

"I can't deal with this right now." She frowns. "I was worried sick, and your dad's been running a fever. Couldn't you at least ring?"

I want to take a shower, change and get to the dance. "I wasn't near a phone."

"Nonsense. You expect me to believe there wasn't one pay phone in whatever bar they let you into?" She shakes her head. "One thing's for certain, you're not going to the dance tonight."

"Come on, Mum. I haven't done anything wrong."

"Gladys," Dad yells again.

"I could strangle you I'm so upset right now," Mum says.

She stamps off to look for the hot water bottle.

The old man is conked out in front of the telly, wads of tin foil glinting from the tips of the antennae. He's waiting for the late news. His legs and arms, bordering on chubbiness, fill out a baggy pair of pin-striped jammies.

He waits for a commercial. "John."

"Ya." I've taken to a kind of monosyllabic language with the embattled king of our homestead.

"Where've you been?"

"Around."

He grunts, and a loud rattle indicates Mum has turned on the kitchen taps.

I stare at the floor.

I don't like to see him like this. The low table in front of him is covered in everything he needs to stay glued to that chair: rolled-up Kleenex, a few slices of lemon, a bottle of nasal spray, and leftover chicken soup. Only an act of God could pry him from this post.

An eternity of ah's later he lets rip a humungous sneeze.

"Kulvinder's mother has been phoning about your work schedule," he finally says.

"I know."

I couldn't give a flying fig about slaving away for Mrs. Sharma at Fawzia's Authentic Indian Cuisine.

"Call her," he sniffles.

"I will."

From his forehead he removes a wet flannel that Mum, no doubt, plonked there.

"It's all about honest effort, Son," he says. "That's all your mother and I expect of you."

"Absolutely, Dad."

Right. I doubt he believes any of this Father Knows Best crap. Look where it got him. Look. Despite honest effort we've spent our years in Vancouver this side of eating out of dustbins.

Anyway, I'm not about to explain myself. There's a school dance to prepare for; Mum can't stop me from going.

Dad stares at the TV, then lapses into silence. I back out of the room while he coughs.

Mum enters my bedroom with a glass of apple juice; hands it over, then squishes down beside me and puts an arm around my shoulders. "John, you must try harder."

I run a pick through my nappy hair.

"Pumpkin." She squeezes closer. "You've always run with the throttle on high. Come on now. Calm down a little. Can't you see we're worried about you?"

"Ah, man."

"It's been rough for all of us lately. You know that."

It hasn't helped that Dad won't follow through on job leads she finds for him. Since the move it's as if Dad's been decked by a wicked uppercut, and he's sitting against the ropes trying to get his head clear.

"Just be grateful we have work," she continues.

"How can you stand it, Mum?" She caretakes a young brat with muscular dystrophy. "After just one ten-hour shift with that kid I'd go nuts."

She laughs. "Son, there's no shame in serving others. Especially when people are dependent on you for their survival."

"Well, I've had it with washing dishes. There are better ways to spend my time."

"Like what, watching television all day with your father?"

I pause for a moment.

Now that I've had a few drinks, Kulvinder's insistence on running track doesn't seem bad. But I know if I mention it, Mum'll go on first about Koech, then my marks at school. I say it anyway. "Run." I'll do anything to get out of that bleeding kitchen. "I was asked to join a track club today by a guy who went to the Olympics."

It's a long shot, I know, but Kulvinder promised to talk Coach Holt into taking me on.

She's quiet for a while. Rock music detonates through the floorboards upstairs while I comb through knots in my hair.

I have no idea how Jugs and Slim manage up there. The mister gets the missus to party with him. They stay up till four in the morning, smoking pot and listening to the collected works of Pink Floyd. Then a round of arguing leads to loud, pre-dawn shagging.

Make no mistake. I'm no prude. I understand some folks need to hit the pipe and crack open a box of sex toys now and again. I just don't want to have to listen to it.

"Is it going to cost, dear?"

"I can pay for most of it with my savings. But I'll need to borrow a bit for some spikes."

It's true. If I get into the club, I'll need an upgrade in gear.

"How much?"

"One hundred and fifty dollars."

"John!"

"I know it's a lot of money, but I'll pay you back."

"I can't keep . . ."

"Okay, forget it."

"It's just you go out drinking till all hours, don't call, and when you get home, you treat me like some sort of bank machine," she says.

"Holy shit, Mum," I blurt out. "I said forget it."

She gets huffy. "You have no right . . . How dare you use that foul language . . . I cannot be around you right now." She leaves.

Fine.

I skim through an article in *Track and Field News* on the eight.

A change of guard has taken place in the event. Coe and Ovett have retired. Cruz, the heir apparent, lost his form after the games in L.A. and now Wilson Kipketer, the Kenyan who migrated to Norway, is the world record holder.

Mum returns. She hands me a stack of cash.

I object. I'm not taking her money.

"Listen, Son. What matters is that you've found something you care about." She pushes 200 dollars into the palm of my hand. "But clean up your act. The police don't need much excuse to put a black person behind bars."

Tears come to my eyes, and the bills in the palm of my hand are blurry. "Thanks, Mum. I'll pay you back." I want to apologize for not coming home earlier, but I clam up. I'm too close to bawling.

"We're going on a picnic Sunday if your dad's feeling better." It's the biweekly family affair at Brighton Park—the one surrounded by factories and bordered by a beach where dead seals wash up.

"Brilliant."

"Be sure not to find another excuse not to come?"

"I'll be there."

"Good. Well, I'm calling it a night. I've taken care of him all day and I'm drained. Would you be a dear and get him some cough syrup?"

I squeeze her arm, then amble shyly off to the sound of "The Wall" caroming through the suite.

I fish around in the medicine cabinet until I get a hold of the Benylin. Then I find a spoon before I take it to the sitting room.

He's propped up with pillows and covered in a blanket as he lies on the sofa and scours the news for reports of events in Kenya.

"Dad." I've been rough on the old man. "I brought you your medicine."

His eyes are yellow, and he wipes at his nose with crumpled toilet paper. "Oh, you brought a teaspoon. I need a tablespoon to take that."

I'd meant to grab the tablespoon, but I'd zoned out. "Why not just take three teaspoons?"

"I need a tablespoon."

If I were Kulvinder I'd just start yelling. I'd say, I've got better things to do with myself than run back and forth getting you a goddamned spoon.

I grind my teeth, swallow, leave and find him his bloody tablespoon.

On my way past their bedroom I see Mum kneeling at an altar. There's a candle on top of a *kitambaa* surrounded by smooth, green pebbles. She burns sage in a bowl and murmurs a prayer to the Knowledge Holders.

4

By the time the folks go to bed, I've lost at least two prime dancing hours. I steal out of the house and wait for Kulvinder at the top of the alley.

"Give me the keys," I demand on his arrival. "I'm driving."

"Don't be daft."

"Listen, if we're going to kill ourselves, I'd prefer to be at the wheel."

"Good Christ." He throws me keys and switches seats. "Let's just get out of here."

I hunch forward, signal, check the rear view mirror for cop cars and inch into the street.

"You can get ticketed for driving too far *under* the speed limit, you know," he says.

I slow down at railroad tracks, check both ways and ease forward.

"Kulvinder." I have to say something. "Don't go downtown on Jugs unless you mean it."

"I'll mean it."

"That's not what I'm getting at. She seems like a nice girl."

"It will cost her a groaning to take off my edge."

Hamlet again.

"Be serious." He can't put a lid on botching quotes from whatever he happens to be reading.

"When was the last time you got laid?" he asks.

I calculate the number of months on fingers.

"It's been ten, mate," he continues. "In contrast, I got a leg up on Helen last weekend."

"That's what I'm talking about."

"That's what I'm talking about."

"Would you stop with the innuendo."

"I'm just speaking to the point."

"The point, there you go again."

He cracks up, hysterically banging the dashboard with his fists.

We arrive at the corny get-down well after midnight.

"Wait here a sec," Kulvinder says before disappearing into the crowded lobby.

I twiddle my thumbs as I stand in my only dressy threads—a scarlet cardigan and navy blue corduroys. Nervous. Hoping my blind date takes to this straight-out-of-the-Sears-catalogue look.

I ought to head to the can for a quick once-over in the mirror.

"Leeds," Kulvinder grabs my arm before I can swing into motion. "Steph and I are going outside."

Jugs has one hand curled around his bicep, and her head is pressed into his shoulder.

"How you doin, Leeds?"

Her words are slurred.

"The usual." If she doesn't have her wits about her, Kulvinder'll roll on her but good. "You?"

"I couldn't be better," she replies.

Svetlana Petrovskaya stands to her left and stares at the strobe lights.

"It's kinda stuffy in here, though," she continues. "So Kulvinder and I are taking a walk."

"Stephanie!" Svetlana exclaims.

I look over their shoulders for my blind date. It couldn't possibly be Svetlana Petrovskaya. She's butch.

"I'll conduct myself like a perfect gentleman," Kulvinder says. "Everything below the knees is off limits."

Jugs doubles over in laughter. "Oh, God." Spit sprays from her lips. "I think I'm gonna pee my pants."

"On that note," Kulvinder announces. "Hillo, ho, ho, good lady! Come, bird, come."

"I hope you guys won't mind holding onto my wallet till we get back?" Jugs wipes tears from her eyes. "It'll give the two of you a chance to talk."

Svetlana!

What are they thinking?

"Remember the golden rule, kids." Kulvinder winks. "Nothing below the knees."

"No sweat," I mutter, grinding my teeth.

Jugs reaches into her pockets and produces keys, lipstick, a tampon and a tiny mirror. She hands these, along with a wallet, to Svetlana. Then they disappear outside.

This isn't good. Svetlana tends to sit at the back of the class, where she pulls on her dark bangs and chews her nails.

Her nose is crooked, and she's on the pudgy side, plus she has a cleft in her chin.

Svetlana's in full chew mode as I stand beside her in the dark dining hall. She's chomping at the quick.

Overplayed standards with familiar hooks jimmie whoops and cheers out of the jacked-up crowd. Boys wearing I'm-with-stupid T-shirts play air guitars and bellow in one another's ears. Girls decorated in Grandma's jewellery move as if it's serious, this dancing business. Bunched in small groups like chattel in a pen. The sober are a collection of prats. Checking digital watches and fingering their pockets for quarters with which to call home.

My temples ache.

I don't know what the hell to say. So, Svetlana, what do you think of . . . I can't fill in the blank.

How could Jugs do me like this?

"Svetlana," I finally shout. "What do you think of the poems we're studying in Finch's class?"

"The best thing one can say about Ezra Pound is that at least he had good enough taste to be involved with Hilda Doolittle."

"Right." Damned if I know what the hell she's talking about. "You must read a lot."

"Don't you?"

"*Othello* wasn't bad."

"You actually *liked* that play?"

"Sort of." I don't want to get into the details. "Forget school. Did Stephanie tell you about the cross-country race?" She yawns. "It's not my specialty, you know. I'm in serious training to . . ." run at the Provincials isn't impressive enough.

". . . break the four-minute mile." Of course, there's more to say about corporate sponsorships and so on. But she's too close to Jugs. Now that she and Kulvinder are hitting it, I have to be careful. Any outrageous lie will bounce back and nick a chunk of flesh out my ass. "If one believes in their dreams and stays off drugs anything is possible."

"It figures," she says.

"What?"

"Sports. Testosterone. It figures."

I shut up, my palms sweaty and a migraine coming on.

The late night DJ from CJLX FM has been playing a steady diet of Supertramp and Styx. Now he's on a Cheap Trick kick.

I'd like to request "Don't Stop till You Get Enough" (Michael Jackson, *Off the Wall*), but I don't have the guts.

If only Kulvinder and Jugs would put a rush on their bonk and join us.

After about 200 years I decide to make a night of it. It's been irritating, standing around guarding Jugs' belongings when we could be out there getting our swerve on.

"Don't you feel Stephanie's taking advantage of you?" I finally ask.

The lines around her mouth converge in dimples. "I could ask you the same thing about Kulvinder."

"You're not comparing my relationship with yours?"

"I just did."

"You know nothing about me."

"Hmmmmm. Let's see, you used to get chauffeured around in European cars before you moved to Canada. Right?"

"Wrong."

"Balderdash," she replies.

"Balderwhat!" I shake with indignation. "For your information I didn't have a childhood. We lived from hand to mouth. Foot to mouth. Whatever the expression is."

Luckily, the DJ slows things down with "It's Over" by Boston. Thank God, a slow jam. Something we can do where we don't have to talk.

"Listen, why don't we just go dance?" I ask.

She pulls on her bangs and looks towards the door. "No."

And that's that.

What a flake. No one in his right mind would put up with what she's putting me through. Kulvinder certainly wouldn't. He'd come right back by going ahead and asking someone else to dance.

"You'll have to excuse me," I say. "I need to use the can."

Holy Jesus. I need to be a different person, a necessary person.

I climb onto the window sill in the crapper, stare at the dark outline of tall, rolling mountains encircling the city, and bring the evening to a halt with a ten-foot leap and drop.

When I get home it's after 2:30. I slide through the back door and tip toe across the shag carpeting to my bedroom.

I can't sleep. The mister and the missus are into Jethro Tull. Next up will be blue films, bigass lines of coke, and hand jobs.

Why Svetlana?

Sure, the bridge of my nose is a little on the broad side and my lips a bit thick. But Svetlana Petrovskaya!

I put on Koech's sweat top, steal into the kitchen and open the fridge. The juice container is empty, and we're out of fruit.

I return to bed. Plug my fingers into my ears. Toss about. Sit up. Wrap myself in a blanket, then go lie down on the sofa in the sitting room.

Outside one of the hookers haggles with a trick.

"Forty for a blow," she says.

"Thirty."

"Forty and ya gotta wear an overcoat."

"Overcoat?"

"Jimmy hat. Condom."

"Thirty."

"This ain't no fuckin auction."

I flee to the bathroom.

Upstairs the mister and missus thrash towards respective orgasms by belting out pet names.

"Cocksucker."

"Cunt."

I turn on the taps in both the sink and the bath.

FLOOOOOSH.

It only creates more thumping in my head.

I hate existing. Hate, hate, hate it. Where the fuck does Svetlana get off thinking she knows the score?

A grubby lining of tar-like film squirms beneath my skin. I reach into the medicine cabinet and rummage around in Dad's shaving kit for a razor.

The blade is clean.

I look for veins in my forearm, settle on a spot in the thick part of my triceps and start to cut.

This world is the complete opposite of the one we've escaped: crowded cement flats plastered in coats of red dust, workers hurrying to hang onto doors of overcrowded buses, Matatus and women strapped with lopsided bundles. Donkeys, stray dogs, Ochieng na mpira on the transistor radio, Ochieng na mpira, Ochieng na mpira, shoot, goooooooooooaaaaaal, goooooooooooaaaaal, blind drunks, lame beggars and polio, muddled prophets, brawls and knife fights, pombe, pangas, bible-thumping street preachers singing hellfire and salvation, stale bread covered with thick margarine, rumours of attempted coups, toys made from discarded wire, and the never-ending speculation surrounding the ones who made it to houses like this one in Langata.

Mind, we have the well-to-do Minister of Finance to thank. He gave Dad a promotion, a raise and an office with swank carpets. Now we can get a Watchman, and a colour telly. Super, eh?

I'm eleven. It's Saturday morning, and I knock about while beefy blokes unload trunks, furniture, and boxes from a lorry. The day is hot as a bleeder, and Dad sweats in the middle of it all, his sleeves rolled up to his elbows. A self-made man wearing stiff khakis and flip-flops that slap the brown earth.

I'm twitchy with excitement. This will be our first house, a humongous stone mansion surrounded by a tall, thorny hedge. Right next to the home of the man who owns Sharma's, a snazzy shop on Moi Avenue, escalators between each of its ten floors.

I park myself on the veranda steps, flick through the pages of a hardcover edition of The Olympiad and pick a scab on my knee. Dad won't let me help because he says moving is for adults.

What rot.

He doesn't mind a hand from Koech, and he just turned sixteen. If only they let me, I could carry some of the smaller chairs into the dining room. Easy.

My brother is a quiet, willowy chap with a tall, spiky Afro. He mimics the work ethic of his Czech idol, Emil Zatopek, by running

twice a day in army boots. It's brilliant. Unfortunately he's met his
match in an antique sofa he heaves towards the house. The sofa's
back legs drag through the grass.

Crikey, if Mum sees him she'll have a fit.

I jump up, sprint over and grab hold of the dragging end.

"Let it alone," Koech pants. "I'm managing fine."

I ignore him, lean forward and lift, but the sofa's velvet backing
is slippery, and I topple backwards onto the mowed lawn.

"Leeds!" Koech shouts in exasperation. "I've got it."

Dad pops his head out of the lorry as I scramble to my feet.

"What did I ask you, John?" he says.

"The sofa was too heavy, and Koech isn't an adult, so I . . ."

"That isn't what I asked."

I get quiet.

"Stay out the way," Dad continues. "Stay, Out, The, Way."

I slump back down on the veranda and fume, a steady parade of
newly purchased Victorian furnishings shuttling past.

After forever, Dad joins me.

"Even lions rest in the shade when it gets too hot," he grumbles.

Koech weighs in. "I can't do much more." He wipes his brow.
"I've got to save something for track workout later."

Dad laughs. "How do you expect to eclipse Kip Keino if you
fold as easily as the rest of us?" he replies. "That man ran with
a gall bladder problem in the Games at Mexico City and still
managed to trounce the American in the 1500."

"Jim Ryun," I blurt.

"Yes, Ryun," Dad says.

Koech sighs, gathers himself together and keeps at it.

I swat at flies attached to the corners of my mouth, then escape
down the veranda steps onto a pebbled path. I pass Dad's yellow
Renault parked in the garage.

A horizontal wooden fence that stretches across the width of the back garden halts my progress. I swing open a gate and walk by the servants' quarters. The building is divided into four rooms around a concrete courtyard; at its centre sits a jiko loaded with charcoal. Behind it a huge vegetable garden extends into a wall topped with broken glass.

Where's the smell coming from?

I drag a rotten bench through overturned soil, termites slithering over my hand.

Then, "Ooo wee, ooo wee, ooo weee." I stop. "Ooooweee, oooweee." On the other side of the wall a woman's cry shakes the stagnant air. "Oooweee, ooowee." I inch the bench closer. "Woooooololo. Woooolo." Set it up against cement and put a foot on it. Before I hoist myself upward, black smoke falls down thick and heavy, wringing tears from my eyes. I stagger backwards, coughing, the sting rooting in my lungs.

I beat a hasty retreat.

By the time I can breathe again, I've stumbled into the front garden, the grass littered with coin-shaped holes where tarantulas hide from the sun. I walk past a swing set and through a narrow opening between rose bushes. Another, much larger, garden is flanked on either side by a dried-up ditch and a wooden fence. I cross over to the Sharma's side and press my face into a football-sized hole in the middle of the fence.

A brown boy with a green turban lounges on a fold-out chair beside a corker of a swimming pool.

"Hello," I shout.

He flips two fingers at me. "Sod off," he yells back.

5

The evening after the dance, Kulvinder and I are twenty minutes late for work at Fawzia's Authentic Indian Cuisine. We sneak into the kitchen through the back door and get busy cleaning out the can. Two of the crappers are plugged, and the floor under the urinals is sticky with piss.

My arms smart where the cotton sleeves stick to my scabs, and I'm hung over. "I think I blew a gasket in my head."

"Don't be such a hypochondriac."

"I'm not," I reply. "There's something majorly wrong with me this time."

"When blood starts oozing out your ear, I'll be the first to call an ambulance."

He grins.

"Right, hearing me out would only add weight to your life."

"Like I said . . ."

When we're done in the can, we scoop leftover slop from stacks of plates, wash dishes and haul rubbish into the skanky alley out back.

Dishes are by far the worst. They're boring as all get out to wash, yet require focus. Broken plates and glasses cost money to replace, cash the higher-ups lift from our paycheques.

I'm careful to avoid looking at the clock.

That's what it takes to make it through the motherfucker. Avoiding and evading, ignoring the fluorescent light. Trying to distance myself from Joginder and his apprentice, Ranjith, who both chop greens and lean dangerously over boiling vats of water.

Joginder's twenty-eight going on forty-five, bloated belly and three rug rats to clothe and feed at home.

Ten years down the line he'll be working his ass off in someone else's kitchen, maybe taking home a dollar fifty more an hour. His major task will be to get through another day without gobbling down a bottle of iodine.

I'm afraid of him. Afraid of going out like that.

"Switch." Kulvinder hands me a dishtowel, shoves me aside and dives elbow-deep into the sink.

I look towards the clock but stop at greasy new shutters on the windows beneath it. It won't do to get ahead of myself. Time won't pass any quicker if I count the hours to see exactly how much I've made.

"Hello, hello?" Kulvinder splashes me with water. "Anyone home?"

I whack him with the dishtowel.

"I told you. I'm hung over."

"Oh, that," he says. "And I thought you were thinking about how shoddily you treated Svetlana last night."

"Not a chance," I reply. "One day that chick's going to plant homemade bombs in the cafeteria. I got nothing to feel bad about."

"You're incorrigible."

"Crikey, why do you have to talk like that?"

"And what, pray tell, should I say instead?"

"How about . . . nasty."

"Incorrigible's more precise."

"Nasty is better."

"Right."

"Anyway, Jugs should never have set me up with Svetlana in the first place."

"Hey, a little respect, her name is Stephanie."

"Come again?"

"Not Jugs," he says. "Stephanie."

"You're not serious."

"Bloody well right I'm serious."

Over in the kiss-ass section, Joginder mutters something catty to Ranjith in Punjabi and frowns.

What a couple of clowns. Ranjith is a sulky little prick who didn't finish high school.

"You and your friend didn't turn off the lights on Thursday night," Ranjith interrupts.

"Is he talking to us?" Kulvinder replies.

Joginder rolls his eyes. "They were still on when I came in Friday morning."

Kulvinder scowls. "Ranjith was last to leave."

"Liar," Ranjith replies.

"You were on the phone with your girlfriend when we left," I remind him.

"Thursday night is your responsibility," Joginder says.

"We weren't last to leave," Kulvinder objects.

Ranjith turns to Joginder. "He only behaves this way because his father was a big wig in Africa." He points at Kulvinder's shaved head. "But what do you expect from someone who's ashamed to be Sikh."

Kulvinder drops his shoulders and rushes towards him. They fold on contact, crumpling to the floor.

I try to jump between them, but Joginder is quick to pull me off and wrestle me into a headlock.

The floor's wet. We slide, flail and twist until I get a hand up to the turban at the top of his head.

"Hey," Joginder says. "Let go."

I hold on and we fall against a counter. Frying pans bounce and skitter along the floor.

"You first," I say tugging hard on the turban.

Joginder tightens his grip around my throat.

There's a mother of an ache where a bone in his forearm presses hard against my Adam's apple, and my forehead burns like it's full of white coals.

I can't breathe. But I'm not about to let go.

"What's going on here?" Kulvinder's old lady stands before us in a pile of shuddering pans, her bangled arms crossed.

"Nothing, Mrs. Sharma." I push Joginder off me.

"Just finishing up some dishes, Mummy." Kulvinder slaps Ranjith's hand away from his neck.

Mrs. Sharma knits a brow shiny with lotion and sucks saliva through her gums. "How many times . . . Joginder, you know I expect you to set a finer example. Listen, we're out of spinach . . . I'm going back to work and I expect the same of you. If not, you'll all be looking for new jobs come morning." She swishes out of the room, the bottom of her red sari tracking carrot shavings behind her.

I can't afford to mess this one up. It'll be the fourth job Kulvinder and I have either quit or been fired from in the past year.

Mrs. Sharma did us a favour when she hired us. We had nowhere else to go. So there are high expectations. Hustle. Move. Mop floors. Unpack produce. Offer to bus a couple of goddamn tables if we have to. But we've been here less than a month, and Kulvinder's already getting in fights.

Kulvinder turns back to the dishes. "Don't ever mention my daddy again, Ranjith."

"Is that supposed to be some sort of threat?"

"Take it any way you want."

"Kulvinder." I rub my neck. "I need this job."

"Listen to your friend," Joginder says.

"Never again," Kulvinder sneers.

We work quietly for a while, juiced on guilt.

Kulvinder sprays hot water onto plates he places in a bucket. "They won't respect us until we make a name for ourselves," he says.

Not this again. I'm not about to get into it with him. Somehow the conversation always precedes a twisted blowout with his mummy. He tells her how unhappy he is and says fuck. She tells him he's an ungrateful child. Tears are shed and doors slammed before the inevitable apologies begin.

It screws with my head, and I'm just glad I never go through anything that demented with my folks.

"Hey, focus on what you're doing," I say, scraping leftover rice into a dustbin. "You've started to miss plates."

"You have to ring up Coach Holt, mate," Kulvinder replies. "He needs to hear from *your* mouth that you want to run.

Think of how brilliant it'll be: newspaper coverage at the big meets, trips all over the country. We'll even meet chicks from places like Toronto."

Bus boys with yellow pit stains shuttle through the doors and drop another load of dishes on us.

"I don't know, man." Now that I'm sober, it doesn't seem like such a hot idea.

"You're not planning to clean out cans for the rest of your life. I know you. Pick up a phone and ring him."

I've just about exhausted most of my other options. Ice hockey's only reward had been prematurely bearded crackers from places like Medicine Hat crushing us into the boards and spitting on us. "Fuck-face. Faggot. Pakki. Coon." All part of the game, I'd been told. It followed in the tradition of Maurice "the Rocket" Richard, who'd put up with getting called a frog back in the game's glory days.

I'd tried out for the basketball team, my first game taking place against a school for the deaf. But I'd roughed up so many members of the hearing-impaired community that an embarrassed coach had me benched by the middle of the first quarter.

I don't want to run marathons. Those guys look anorexic.

"And think of the soirées afterwards." Kulvinder sprays a batch of glasses with hot water, places them in a bucket and turns to spray another. "We're going to be seventeen soon. If we don't get onto it, we'll never amount to jackshit."

"Could we change the subject? I'm too hung over to think straight."

"Coherently."

"Whatever."

"All right." He stares at a new pile of dishes slated for the sink. "What would Koech do?"

I go for a four-mile run with Koech. It's one of his easy days, but I struggle to keep up as his boots land with a clomp in the dusty lane.

Up ahead a fossil of a man picks through a rubbish bin. His bones stick out at odd places, and loose skin jiggles like a sheet blowing back and forth on the wash line.

"Shikamuu," Koech says waving at him.

"Marahaba," the man replies.

I also wave, although I feel shy about it.

Koech picks up the pace, and I pump my arms hard to stay with his sudden surge. "Quarter of a mile to go."

He glances over at me, grins and opens up a twenty-five-metre gap.

By the time I finish, I'm buggy-eyed and leaning against the front gate.

6

After school the next day, I go to the loading bay at the supermarket. Coach Holt lifts crates of leafy greens, tomatoes and cucumbers out of a refrigerated truck. A teenager wearing a red apron gives him a hand.

"That should just about do her," the youngster says.

"For another week at least." Coach Holt rubs his own shoulders. "Let's break for supper, Justin. We can return the empty crates after."

"I'm working through today, dude," Justin replies. "There are still boxes piled up beside the freezer. I'll get 'em. Got to toughen up for football season, y'know."

"Suit yourself, buddy."

Coach Holt hauls himself away and sits on a knoll of grass. I follow him.

"Excuse me, Coach Holt." I stand in front of him.

He lights up a Players Light. "Eighth place at the cross-country championships, right." I nod. "God, I hate light cigarettes." He inhales. "Doctors! Mine says my cholesterol levels are high, which puts me at risk for a stroke. Oh, don't look so alarmed. All I need to do is stay on a decent diet. I had a small serving of oatmeal for breakfast, these Players Lights are lunch, and my wife, Kioko, will come up with some seaweed concoction for dinner." He laughs.

"Look, Coach Holt . . ." how to put this? ". . . I may not be the biggest or the fastest athlete around . . ." I try to recall what Kulvinder told me to say. "But if you'll be my coach, I'll give you 110 percent effort each and every day."

He looks down at his gut. "Is that so?"

"I know I can do better. I know it."

"Any concrete plans?"

"Come again?"

"Where do you see yourself long-term?"

I improvise. "Getting a track scholarship to a school in the States and running at the Olympics."

He smiles. "Justin never lets up." He staggers to his feet. "I've got to get moving if I'm going to lose twenty pounds this month." He cracks his knuckles. "Come to our first team meeting on Sunday. See what you think, then we'll talk."

Too bad. I kind of hoped for a snag.

He walks back to the store, picks up a load of crates and throws them into the back of a truck. By the second load he stops for a nicotine break.

"Hurry it up," Justin says. "You're slowing us down."

The following week Kioko Holt, Coach's second wife, leads Kulvinder and me into the basement of a posh little aluminum siding number.

She's a loopy, dramatic Japanese woman. Nice teeth and a killer set of curly eyelashes.

"Welcome," she shouts, herding us downstairs into the basement. "Welcome."

The walls are covered in track medals and the shelves stacked with trophies. There's a snapshot of Coach in a 400-metre hurdle heat at the L.A. Games, FloJo's Games, the ones the Soviet Bloc didn't bother showing up for. This photo hangs beside another of him clearing a hurdle years before, a red headband snugly binding a puffy Afro.

He arranges a file full of papers on a table at the back of the room. From the looks of it, he was once a tall and sinewy man. But now his hair is reduced to tufts at his ears, and he boasts an unhealthily healthy gut.

A light-brown sister in oversize overalls curls up on a sofa. Ripped arms clasp her legs. Her hair is cropped tightly to her skull. Erica Upton. A real big-shot on the track scene. On display in front of the Vogue on Granville Street, is an ad with her cozying up to an oversized container of hand cream. A second cola-dark sister sits at the opposite end of the couch. She's leggy, and her hair runs buck wild in braided chaos at the top of her head.

Brilliant. Nobody mentioned training with a couple of lookers.

It's difficult to say what makes them such dishes. They're just . . .

"Sit." Kioko whirls her arms about in the four directions. "Sit."

"Thank you, Mrs. Holt," Kulvinder says.

We squeeze in between the sisters. Getting a bucketful of body contact to boot.

"Yes, thanks, Mrs. Holt," I chime in.

"That's Kioko," she says. "The only missus is my mother and she lives in Tokyo."

Coach works his way over to her, flings his arms around her waist and slops a noisy kiss on her neck.

"Sam," she protests. "You'll have to save that for later. I'm going upstairs to finish canning the peaches."

"Right on, Kiki." He slaps her playfully on the ass.

"Later," she says giggling.

It is, to be honest, a little embarrassing. But he's an Olympian. They have trophy cabinets filled with important photos.

Coach Holt kicks things off with introductions. We're to refer to him at all times as Sam, and the looker with the wild hair is Vivian Sawyer. We all say what's up and smile before Sam shifts into a rap on high performance athletics.

"If you're going to make it to the top," he says, "it'll require commitment. You'll have to work harder than you've ever worked before. There will be days when you'll wake up in the morning too sore to get out of bed. Dog tired. But this, as you will learn, will also be life offering you an invitation, one that asks if you are willing to take that next step. That big step on a road travelled only by a courageous few." That's exactly what he said. Saliva began to gather on the ridges of the roof of my mouth. "To be a winner," he reads from one of his pieces of paper, "the athlete must accept pain—not only accept it but look for it, live with it, learn not to fear it.

"I've had some great talent. Erica will tell you. Todd Payne, who's at Michigan State. Renee Hammond at North Carolina. That could be any one of you next year. But it won't come easy. You'll have to start by taking control of your life. Never write a cheque with your tongue that you cannot cash with your conduct. Never underestimate the power of affirmative thinking."

He lights up a John Players Special, takes a puff then rolls back into his spiel.

"It was said that John Akii Bua, the great Ugandan hurdler, never got nervous before a race. Why? Because he always showed up knowing there was nobody in the field better prepared. If you fail to prepare, you prepare to fail."

He discards his cigarette in an ashtray, props a board up on a chair by the wall and scribbles out a diagram. Proving, to me anyway, that he not only knows his stuff but also has a scientific basis for it. Make no mistake; his smoking throws me a little. But we aren't kids anymore. People smoke. It doesn't have to mean more than that.

"We, like this great runner, will be expected to follow a rigorous program. Phase one will be made up of two runs a day during the week: a long run in the a.m. followed by long intervals in the evening. Saturday is a rest day and Sunday is reserved for a medium paced twelve-mile jog."

On his diagram are a couple of chicken scratches that I can't make any sense of. But what the hell! I get the gist of it. If we sign on the dotted line, we'll be his, a proposition that doesn't seem half bad.

"Oh, I need you to copy down a mission statement to which you must add your own thoughts. You'll hand it in to me by our first group workout next Monday."

Then he goes back to his scribbling.

"Phase two will be an introduction to hills and higher-quality intervals. This will build our anaerobic lactate capacity, our speed endurance. We'll get our mileage in by continuing the daily morning runs. The indoor season won't be a focus. Instead we'll concentrate on peaking in the summer; phase three will be geared towards this end. Mileage will be reduced while we emphasize short, quick intervals with limited recovery."

He straightens out, and I glance over at Kulvinder. His eyes are glazed with tears.

"I expect you to keep a training log, one I will collect at the end of each fortnight. Any questions? All right, we'll watch a documentary on Peter Snell, the great middle distance runner from New Zealand. It examines his relationship with his coach, Arthur Lydiard. But, as you watch it, I want you to remember one thing: I can teach you to run fast, but you must teach yourself to win."

After watching the documentary, Sam takes me aside. "You've got some work to do before I'm convinced you belong in the group." He puts a hand on my shoulder. "You'll start out on a trial basis, and we'll assess your progress three months down the pike."

The following Monday I get up at 6:30 for an easy six-miler. Take a lukewarm shower, have a quick bowl of Cheerios, then wait at the bus stop with Jugs, a half-dozen mother-daughter combos from Hong Kong and the neighbourhood hos who flag down the station wagons that circle the block.

Jugs and I sit in the physically handicapped and oldster seating at the front, the endorphins kicking in to make her seem all the more fetching and babelicious.

The morning run was a breeze, and I focus on the first group workout this evening.

Unfortunately, Jugs is a bit of a wrench in the works. She smells of coconut butter, and I'm tempted to plant my tongue in her ear. Or worse yet, to tell her that I'm tempted to plant my tongue in her ear.

Whoa. Get a grip.

I kick into classy mode by eliminating cheeky brushes against her bare skin and keeping chitchat primed with choice observations on the twits we suffer through school with.

"Little has changed in the time I've known them." I chuckle. "All they do is complain about millionaire developers from Hong Kong muscling in on the city with butt-ugly monster homes." I give her a moment to absorb it all.

She takes it in as if I'm a twat. Her eyebrows arch and her pouty lips freeze open.

I don't get it. It isn't as if I'm talking twaddle.

I suppose my hair could use a work-up. A conk. A sweet set of dreads. Something that would keep her attention, no matter what sort of blather comes tumbling out my trap.

Kulvinder gets on the bus, plunks himself down beside her and turns down the volume on his Walkman.

"There's a cut you've got to hear, luv," he says to her.

"Love. I like that." She twirls a finger in her hair. "What you listening to?"

"Ice T."

Kulvinder gives Jugs one of his headphones, smacks a wet kiss onto her lips and turns up the music.

I can hear them sample a bunch of "motherfucking motherfucks" coming out of the profanely cool mouth of Ice T. My forehead smudges the window with face cream while I examine their reflection.

Kulvinder and I take the Chevy to track practice as soon as school's out. The day solidly behind us as we plot and plan our way to world domination in the eight.

We figure we'll need to break 1.50 if we're going to get recruited by an American school. Most of the top recruits have run in the low 1.47's.

"Do you think Koech could have beaten Coe?" I ask.

"Forget Coe. What about Cruz?"

"It's tough to say. Cruz never lived up to his potential. He was a lot like that Cuban 400-metre runner with the great-looking Afro and long white socks. Juantor whatshisname."

"Juantorena."

"Yeah, like him," I say. "Tall. Lanky. Strong. World class 400-metre speed. Susceptible to lower leg injuries."

"Cruz ran something like 1.44 when he was a junior."

"He never broke Coe's world record though."

"That's 'cause his coach moved him up to the fifteen too fast," he replies.

"You think so."

"Yeh. But he still ran 1.41.7. That isn't fooling around."

"Sure. But I bet Koech can run that fast."

Rush hour traffic on Hastings Street fucks with the forward momentum of the Chevy. At the intersection on Abbott Street we inch past six cops who oversee a film crew scouring the grimy sidewalk. Beyond them actors are dressed like high-class whores: short bright skirts, skintight tube tops. Dark stockings above pastel-coloured heels.

Slowly, we make our way past more cops at the back end of the shoot. Then we're back among a mishmash of locals, stuck to the dusty sidewalks like discarded wads of chewing gum.

We're supposed to meet in a parking lot in Stanley Park at five. But we get there a couple of minutes late.

"Practice starts at five o'clock," Sam says. "Not five-oh-four but five o'clock." Erica and Vivian are already stretching under spruce trees. "The warm-up is one of the most impor-tant parts of our training regimen. Can you tell us why, Erica?"

"To help us steer clear of injuries."

"To help us steer clear of injuries." It seems as if they're sharing some kind of joke. "We don't want to start the season by developing nasty problems with shin splints." We nod bash-fully. "So I need you to be here on time and to put in a good forty-five-minute warm-up before the workout gets under way."

I hand in my mission statement. A three-page letter outlin-ing, in detail, why I'll turn out to be such a goddamned asset to the fold. Then he sends us off on a ten-minute jog.

We lag behind the girls as we run in an open field. Gaggles of geese feed on the grass, and we tramp through their soft green turds.

Tourists take snapshots of cedar totems, cone-rich firs and tall flat-needled hemlocks, their ass-backward presence offset by the distant sound of cars gathering along Georgia Street for an assault on the Lions Gate Bridge.

I have to make up for such a piss-poor start. If I work real hard, I'll redeem myself.

On our return Sam takes us through a series of stretches. "This one is good for the hams." We partner up. Kulvinder lies on his back and rests one leg on my shoulder before resisting as I push against it. "Careful," Sam says. "You want to stretch not tear his hamstring." After fifteen seconds Kulvinder switches legs. Then it's my turn.

I'm embarrassed by how inflexible I am. Especially because both Erica and Vivian can push one another's legs into a 140-degree angle without strain. "Edwin Moses stretched up to six hours a day in his prime," Sam comments. "The boys could take a page out of his book."

We do several more stretches as Sam continues to point out their function. "This one is for the glutes," or, "that one is for the quads." Then it's time for drills and high knee lifts.

I can't quite get the coordination down. There are too many technicalities to keep on top of. "Keep your arms at a ninety-degree angle and move them forward as if they were pistons. Good, Vivian. Now watch the knees. WATCH THE KNEES. High lifts. High lifts."

I'd be humiliated as heck if Kulvinder weren't all over the place as well.

We finish the warm-up with five one-hundred-metre accelerations.

"I want you to keep in mind all that we worked on during the drills. Stay relaxed and make sure you're running close to full speed by about eighty metres. Any questions?"

It sounds simple enough. Relax and accelerate. But as soon as we hit thirty metres, I'm lost. It doesn't make any sense. Whenever I press, I tighten up. When I relax, I slow down. "Leeds, don't cock your head to the right like that. Think tall and stop grimacing as you approach top speed. Relax the face. No. Relax. RELAX."

I'm butchered by the time I'm done. This relaxation business is hard work. The workout hasn't even started yet, and I'm ready to pack it in.

"We'll ease into things today with six sets of 2000-metre intervals with about a six-minute jog between each. Each interval should be at approximately seventy-five percent effort. That's seventy-five percent, people. Not sixty percent or ninety percent. But seventy-five percent." He looks at a stopwatch that hangs around his neck. "I want Erica to put her arm up when you're ready to begin and drop it when you start."

We gather beside a lamp post near the top of a bike trail. Then we're away.

The first one's a cinch. I'm running up there with the others at what feels like seventy-five percent effort.

"Kulvinder and Leeds, I said seventy-five percent. Not fifty percent." Sam shakes his head.

"I could have pressed a little harder," I reply. "But . . ."

"No excuses," Sam snaps. "Just do it right this time."

Ouch. That hurts. It's easy for a coach. He only has to stand there and boss people about. Go fast. Lift your legs. Don't cock your head.

Kulvinder and I press harder on the second one; both Vivian and Erica stay with us even when we surge over the final 250 metres.

Sam shakes his head again when we come through the finish. "Good work, ladies," he says.

Kulvinder begins to press even more during the next couple, and I stay with him. But there's no way we're at seventy-five percent. Sure we drop the girls. But what's the point of Sam telling us to run one way before forcing us to do it another?

By the time we hit the fifth one, my legs feel like rubber and I begin a slow painful-ass fade at the halfway mark. It's awful, and I'm shuffling a little faster than a brisk walk near the finish.

I wind up about fifty metres behind Kulvinder and fifteen metres behind Erica.

At the finish I double over, panting in front of Sam.

"Remember," he says. "He who is just coasting along has to be going downhill."

The last one is even worse than the one before. Even Vivian moves past me with 500 metres to go.

"That was a good start." We lie gasping on the grass, which is covered in goose shit. "We'll be doing many more of this type of session in the months to come."

When Kulvinder and I get into his car, I'm still hurting. I put up the hood of Koech's sweat top and don't say a word.

"I can't keep doing this," he interrupts.

"What?"

"Carrying you."

I'm shocked. "It was my first workout with the squad, for crying out loud."

"I saw the cuts on your arms." I stare out the window. "Wake up, mate. People are starting to notice."

"People? Which people?"

"Steph for one," he says. "She's worried you'll do something daft."

"I haven't . . ."

"Christ, if you want to kill yourself, just do it. Get it over with. Otherwise, start making an effort."

My voice begins to shake. "An effort! What do you think I've been doing?" I watch his fingers tighten around the steering wheel. "You have no idea what it's like." His life moves easily in the directions he wants it to take. "You think you know. But you have no clue."

"You're not getting any pity here, Leeds," he replies. "Either shit or get off the pot."

I look through the fence. The brown boy lies on his back with a comic over his face.

"Hey, you."

He lazily lifts one edge of the strip.

"What's your name?" I ask.

"Who wants to know?"

"Leeds."

"Ha. What kind of poncey name is that?"

"It isn't poncey."

"Keep your tits on, mate." He stresses his p's and t's. "Mine is Arsenal."

"Really."

"Ha. Not a chance. I'm Kulvinder."

He stands, wraps his waist in a blue towel and walks towards me. Crumbs! He's got muscles.

"What does your daddy do?" He asks.

"He's in the government." I emphasize my n and t.

"See the smoke?" Kulvinder points to the back of our house. "It's from the slum."

"The slum?"

"That's where the natives live." His voice gets real low. "We're getting a dog for protection."

"Natives?" They live in the bush.

"Natives," he repeats. "Don't you know anything?"

"Natives." I imitate the way he draws out the a. Neiiiightives. Those people have bones in their noses and ivory plates jutting out of their bottom lips.

"Stop talking like a moron."

"Take that back," I yell.

"Blimey," he replies. "You're a touchy bloke."

"Don't call me a moron. I'm going to Ginger Academy."

He pauses. "You going to school at Ginger Academy?"

"Yeh."

"That's where I go."

"Yeh, you heard of Sports Day?"

"Of course," he says. "I'm going to win the 200 again this year."

"Swank."

"Who'll beat me? You?"

I didn't plan to race. "My big brother says anybody can be beat." Koech is the runner in the family.

"No native can beat me in a sprint," he says. "You can run the long distances, but anything below the mile is too short."

Rubbish, I think. But I can't come up with the name of a Kenyan sprinter who medalled at the Games. "I'm no native."

7

It's 7:40 in the morning. My body aches, and I'm exhausted from a night disrupted by leg cramps and arguing between the mister and the missus upstairs.

Twenty minutes. I have twenty minutes to make it to the bus stop.

Gingerly I place the balls of my feet on the cold floor.

"Shit." I use my hands for support, slowly lifting myself upright. "Shit. Oh, shit." One shockwave rips through my calves, another through my hamstrings and up into my buttocks; the pain migrates up my back and finds itself a grazing spot in my temples.

I shuffle out of my pyjamas, struggle into jeans and groan all the way to the bathroom, where the soft bristles of the toothbrush hurt my gums.

"Are you okay, sweetheart?" Mum asks.

I manoeuvre into a wooden chair at the breakfast table.

I can only put pressure on my left bum cheek.

"Yeah. Yes. Sure."

Dad stands and glares out the window. "That fellow with the white Fiat is parked in front of our house again."

"Leave it be, Ahab," Mum says. "We don't even use the spot."

"This is the third day in a row."

"Come and have your breakfast. You can worry about that sort of thing when you get yourself a car."

Dad mutters to himself before joining us. "Pass the cereal," he says.

"You really mustn't overdo it, Son," Mum says.

"I'm fine," I snap. Why won't she back off? "It's a bit of an adjustment is all."

"You have five minutes to get to the bus stop," Dad grumbles. "Five minutes."

I can hear the monologue going on in his head. *You can't talk any sense to the boy. He's trying to be like Koech, but he's deluding himself. It's a shame to see him waste his energy on a pipe dream. He ought to just buckle down at school.*

"Our son hasn't finished eating, Ahab."

"He'll miss the bus."

"Let him eat in peace. He'll get there on time." She winks at me and stuffs a cellophane bag filled with bologna sandwiches into my knapsack.

It's her day off.

It makes me nuts. She needs to sleep in. Watch a soap if she has to. Call someone about the Teaching Certificate she talks of re-taking because she isn't allowed to teach in Canada with the one she has. But there are groceries to buy, floors to clean, laundry to be done, and if she doesn't do it . . .

"I should go," I say.

"If you see that *Wazungu* with the Fiat, tell him he's parked in our spot," Dad says.

"Have a good day, John!"

"Later, Mum."

I labour out the door, making sure my clothes don't make any contact with my skin.

Jugs babbles when I see her. "I don't want you to get it wrong." She's talked to Kulvinder. "I'm into you. Don't think any different. It's just I had a friend, Stephanie. Isn't that bugged? People was always tripping around us. That's why I'm Steph and she's Stephanie. Well, Stephanie went to the nut house for a while. That's all I was saying. About Stephanie, and she had problems, and they locked her up."

"Forget it." I get on the bus.

"I didn't sleep from worrying about what you mighta thought of me. I ain't about that. I always got my friends' back. Even when Stephanie said she was, like, into Satan. I only told Colin, my ex. He was the one that ratted her out to the principal. I never did."

"Don't sweat it," I reply. "I'll be checked into a loony bin by noon."

"I never said . . ."

"It really doesn't matter," I say. "Honest."

"Cool." She drops her head onto my shoulder and shuts her eyes. "I want us to chill together, you, Kulvinder and me. Him and I wanna check out a couple of gigs in L.A. this summer. Come. It'll be like . . . what's that bigass rap tour they had . . ."

"Def Jam."

"Yeah, like going to that."

I should run a nasty guilt trip on her. After all she chose Kulvinder over me. But I still have a soft spot for her. This is evident when the tickle of her hair causes the top of my head to sputter like a faulty electrical socket.

"L.A." I reply. "That'd be nice." That is, without Kulvinder.

"By the way, I hope Ma and her boyfriend didn't keep you up late with their fighting."

"Wait a sec, I thought he was your dad."

"Nah. Pa split when Slim was a baby. Larry's just the guy she's shacking up with."

"Man, that's got to be rough." I'm careful not to say more. After all, consoling her on such matters is Kulvinder's territory. Although I don't see why I should give a damn. I'm still pissed at him. The bastard thinks he's got me figured out, and that, more than anything, ticks me off.

"Oh, it ain't too bad," she says. "Slim's the one who takes it hard. He still gets kinda attached to the assholes she brings home. Anyway, that's old. Listen, I just hadda brainwave. Come over tonight. Nobody's gonna be around." She smiles. "Do you like potato salad? We've got loads left over from the weekend."

"I'm not sure . . ."

"It'll be just like when the First Nations, Native People or whatever, make peace. Except we won't smoke a pipe, we'll eat potato salad."

Before I get a chance to answer, Kulvinder struggles onto the bus.

"Hey, love." Jugs shifts over to another seat. "Feel any better?"

"Nah," Kulvinder replies. "I'm sorer than I was last night."

"Poor thing." She leans on him.

"Fuck, Steph! That hurts."

"Sorry." She sits upright and rubs his shoulders.

"Don't," he shrugs. "You're wrinkling my shirt." It's a new black silk number. "Damn, we'll never be able to sustain this load. It's too much. We can't go to school, get our homework done, do our workouts and work at the restaurant four nights a week."

I ignore him.

"I'd really like to come out and watch whatever it is you all do," Jugs says.

"It's boring," Kulvinder replies. "Isn't that right, mate?"

I shrug.

"I don't care," Steph says. "I still want to come."

School is a real downer. This being the day I'm in and out of science labs.

I hate it.

The only class I like is English, where I get to do a presentation on *Othello* tomorrow. I've read the play twice, gone over a gazillion footnotes and flipped through a copy of *Coles Notes*. It's the first time we've studied a book with a black character, and I'm stoked.

However, I think about one thing all day, potato salad with Jugs.

After school I go for a gentle run back home, then boil enough water to take a hot bath.

Jugs and I sit on the front stairs, eating potato salad and rubbing our bare feet into the grass. Over the fence, whores niced-up in outfits from Zellers march from one corner of the block to the other. They mingle with sullen kids, wearing laceless Nikes, off to peddle dope downtown.

I point to a harried-looking bloke muttering on the curb. "He spends all his time picking at sores on his face."

"AIDS."

"Could be anything," I reply. "Some of these folks will stick just about anything into their bodies for a high."

"You got that right," she says. "But it ain't just them. My brother, Slim, got into gasoline last year."

"The squirt!"

"That's why we moved from Calgary," she says. "Social Services wanted to grab him up."

"Crikey!"

"Before that we was on my gramp's farm, which had billions of cats."

"Hmmm."

"The farm belonged to Gramp's pa, who got it free when he moved from England."

"Free land?"

"Crazy, eh? Grandpa says the government usedta give farms away to get white folks to move to Canada."

"Why don't you still live there?"

"It went broke and we moved to Calgary."

"And your grandparents?"

"They're dead."

"Sorry."

"You do drugs?"

"What?"

"Dope."

"Who doesn't?" I lie. "Coke is my thing, though. You know, like Little Richard. Waa baba loo bam . . ."

"Bala bam boom." She laughs. "You're cute when you lie." She reaches to twirl a finger in her hair but ends up spilling potato salad onto her lap. "Shit."

"Here." I hand her a napkin.

"I'm gonna have to change outta these Levis." She stands. "Come on inside."

I follow her indoors and wait in the living room while she disappears to her bedroom. She returns wearing a purple brassiere with matching lace panties. "I can't make up my mind." She holds up a black dress in one hand and some overalls with a T-shirt in the other.

I stare at the carpet. "The overalls."

"You ain't looking."

I raise my eyes. Her flat belly is watered-down beige and darkens where it meets a tuft of protruding pubic hair. "If I didn't know any better, I'd think you were flirting with me."

"Me!" she exclaims. "Don't think I ain't noticed how you make eyes at me."

I gulp. "Not true."

She walks into the kitchen, returns with beer and a bottle of blue pills, then sits beside me on the sofa.

"Anyway, you're not my type," I continue.

"Really. And who is?"

"Well, take Svetlana . . ."

She chuckles and pops two pills. "Have one. It's a nasty buzz."

"No," I reply. "I shouldn't even be drinking. I promised my mum."

"Choirboy." She lays her head in my lap. "Is this cool?"

"Copacetic." I stare down at a bra that reveals the outline of large nipples.

"Wanna know what I'm most scared of?" she finally asks. "Being that guy that picks sores off his face."

"That isn't happening anytime soon."

"I dunno. Everything always goes downhill for me."

I stroke her hair.

She sighs, drifting off on another topic: Kulvinder, and how he's into her one day but treats her like she doesn't exist the next. "He doesn't wanna talk about anything real. I try an' accept that's who he is, but it ain't easy. It makes me jumpy, and I get all wick-whack around him."

"Don't sweat it, Steph. He's an athlete. You just have to make allowances for the craziness in that."

"Sorry," she says. "I didn't mean to get into any of this."

I'm tanked on four Heinekens. "It's okay." What okay means, I'm not sure. "Kulvinder can be a right asshole some-times."

"You don't think less of me?"

"Come on."

"You sure?"

"Well, maybe a little."

She laughs, slugging my arm. Then we stare at one another, and I'm nervous.

"There's always so much going on inside of me," she finally blurts. "Like right now. All I want is to be close, but Kulvinder . . . and I know I shouldn't think of you this way. I know this isn't cool. But I can't help it, 'cause it's myself. Know what I mean?"

The light from the kitchen falls between us onto the sofa. "I'm a wreck half the time, Steph."

She half-laughs. Then tries to deflate the seriousness of the moment by spraying me with beer.

I grab for the can and hold onto her wrist. Her hands are small.

We breathe heavily, then she gives me a long look.

Her corneas are subtly reddening.

When I touch the back of my hand to her cheek, keys jingle at the front door. "Bloody hell." My fingertips turn cold. "Your folks."

"Fuck 'em." She kisses me on the mouth and untucks my shirt.

"No," I push her away. "No."

"Stephanie," her old lady shouts from outside. "Why is the chain on the door?"

"I'll be right there, Ma."

"You better not be fucking around with my home-grown."

I kiss Jugs on the forehead before scampering out her bedroom window.

8

I go for a morning run among newspapers, flattened cardboard boxes and bags of potato chips.

I've my sights set on two schools. Henry Rono went to Washington State and Cruz was at Oregon. If I keep it tight and run fast times early, at least one college should come forward with an offer.

But none of this'll happen if I don't keep my dick in check.

Up ahead an upper-mid lifer jogs off an extended sabbatical from exercise in a fuzzy turquoise jumpsuit. He looks at his watch, his chunky legs churning away productively.

I zero in. Time to separate the men from the also-rans. Children, please leave the room.

I pull up behind him and watch how much energy he's expending, my eyes on the way his legs kick it up a gear. I wait until his steps get choppier before I pounce. Bold. Clean. Decisive. Looking back to savour the sight of him checking his skyrocketing heart rate.

Unfortunately, a little less than a mile later, my legs seize up and I slow down to an eight-minute crawl.

I turn back two miles early and head home, wishing I hadn't pushed myself that hard.

The problem is I just don't know how to try. I get distracted easily or set limits on how hard I push myself. Strange defects I don't know how to control. At a certain point my system shuts down, and I'm just coasting along.

None of the other athletes have these sorts of concerns. The girls, for instance, are a couple of tough fucks.

Erica constantly pushes the pace no matter what the workout is. A strategy that screws me up royally because each practice is more like a race.

Vivian, on the other hand, is potty-mouthed and brash. She spits or burps while we run and says things like, "That was a bitch," after a particularly brutal session.

Both of them have insanely high tolerance levels for pain. Sam could shove bamboo shoots under their nails, and neither one would so much as whimper. They'd merely ask him how many more repetitions of the exercise he'd like them to do.

Erica, who lives in a condo her parents bought her in Kitsilano, appears to be the more talented one. She passed up a full ride at Stanford and chose the University of British Columbia in order to train with Sam. Man, can she burn. She's a lot like Cruz. Wicked 400-metre speed and, at eighteen, still a novice at the event. Her best is an impressive 2.04.73 run in the summer.

She's a bit of a hen-pecker though. Carefully nurturing us while we take our first, tentative steps into track world. "Make sure you consistently get at least eight hours sleep," she nags. Or, "Don't get tempted to look too far down the turnpike. Take it one workout at a time."

Kulvinder can't stand it. He hates being coddled. So he responds by acting extra mature around her.

Vivian's tougher to read. She's a year younger than Erica and runs the 400-metre hurdles. Her best, 57.08.

Not bad at all.

When I hit the top of my block, I walk. It's time to set aside thoughts about messing around with Jugs. I have to focus on the tasty prospect of going to school in the States.

Today English is right after lunch.

Mr. Finch has given us one of two options. Either write an essay or do an oral presentation on a topic of our choice. I dig his style, off the cuff. Always coming up with spur of the moment assignments that make him cooler than any of the other teachers.

He's still on the youngish side and has one of those stushy dos where his rug is swished across his forehead. He never wears suits either; sticks to corduroys and open-necked dress shirts with button-down collars.

The girls love him. Or make that, we're all in love with him. But it's the girls who seem to get the extra attention during recess and after school.

Of course that doesn't mean they're doing the nasty. No such thing. He's married, and Mrs. Finch is expecting their second child.

I stand with quaking hands before my classmates. Take a deep breath. Then hit 'em with it down low.

"Shakespeare is a racist," I begin, and then dish out the real deal for what seems like an hour. Gaining courage as I go along because Finch smiles whenever I look up.

". . . In conclusion," I eventually state, "Shakespeare uses the colour black to convey a theme, as it were, which speaks of the damaging impact of evil on virtue. Take the 'black ram tupping the white ewe,' as a for-instance. Here we have an image that makes the love between Othello and Desdemona something filthy. Iago is angered by this miscegenation, so to speak, and shows his unhappiness by emphasizing the—quote—polarities of good (white) desecrated by evil (black)—unquote. If Shakespeare had meant this play to show us how wrong racism is, the ending would have been different. He wouldn't have made Othello such a hideous beast."

My peers stare back at me with enthused disinterest. Only Kulvinder puts up his hand. Thank God.

"I agree with Leeds." He's coming through for me, and I'm grateful. "Othello can't master his passions. A stereotype. One that makes him an easy target for Iago, the rational white man. This is hardly the mettle of so-called great literature."

I like it when we say "as it were" or "so-called" in front of Finch. It makes us seem more intelligent.

"I couldn't agree more," I add. "Othello is nothing more than a big, passionate black oaf."

The bell interrupts me.

Finch stops me on my way out.

"One cannot apply standards of the late twentieth century to that particular time," he comments. "These things must be read in context. But, that said, you certainly raise a perspective that is refreshing. In fact, come to think of it, there are a couple of novels you should check out of the library. They might help you sort through some of the ideas you brought up." *Black Boy* is the title of a book I can make out at the top of the list. "I'd also like you to do another presentation for your final mark. Or should I say a co-presentation. Svetlana Petrovskaya wrote a delightful paper on *The Crucible* by Arthur Miller. Her take on the witch burnings is one that complements the direction you've begun to explore. I have some time after school; both of you should come see me. We'll discuss this further."

Nooooo. Not Svetlana.

But what is there to be done? Finch is, after all, the teacher. Once they get their minds made up, they stop listening.

Finch is late, and I'm stuck waiting with Svetlana. We sit in desks on opposite sides of his classroom.

"Can I see your arms?" she asks.

"What the fuck!"

"Don't spazz out."

Jugs is a jerk. "They're just arms."

"I haven't told anyone."

"There's nothing to tell," I raise my voice. "Jesus. Can I see *your* arms?"

"I shouldn't have said anything."

"What kind of question is that?"

"I'm sorry."

"They're just arms, for Christ sake."

"I'm sorry. I didn't mean anything." She has tears in her eyes. "I won't bring it up again."

My brain flip-flops, and I can't recall what Finch says on his arrival.

When he's done, I hurry to the locker room, change into my track gear and make a break for the front door. The only way I'll make it to practice on time is if I catch the 4:30.

As I skidaddle down the steps towards the parking lot, I can see the bus approach the school.

"God freakin damn to hell." Svetlana is hitting her handlebars with her fists. "My flicking bike light. Someone lifted my flicking bike light."

"I got a bus to catch."

"Papa will kill me if I don't find that light."

"Shame," I say.

"Holy Mother of Jesus. I'm screwed."

I stop. "Listen, it's just a light." The bus closes in on the stop. "Aren't you overdoing it?"

"You don't know Papa," she mumbles.

"Did you check lost and found?"

"No shit, Eisenstein," she snaps. "It's the first place I looked. Some flicking freak lifted it."

"I have to take off."

Svetlana looks weepy, gnaws on the sleeve of her baggy black sweater and walks back towards the front stairs. She searches blindly all around her.

She's genuinely freaked.

Bugger.

I grit my teeth and go help her.

We look in a flower bed, scan linoleum floors and rummage through dustbins. By the time we get to her locker, the bus is long gone.

Sam will be pissed.

Svetlana looks in her locker under a pile of books that aren't on the curriculum. Perched on the top is a hardback by a woman named Mary Daly.

"Maybe you left it at home," I say.

"I had it with me this morning. I remember that much at least. I'm not a dolt."

All right already. I'm only trying to help.

I notice that she's pasted magazine pictures on the inside of her locker. They're a sorry collection of every possible depressing photograph imaginable. Brown skin hangs like skimpy cloth over living carcasses, eyeballs like giant marbles poke out of sockets, bones are piled in gaping lime pits and so on.

Paper, shards of wood, sheets of corrugated iron and a headless doll surround huge slabs of busted concrete. People mill around cardboard shacks, dust settling on their twisted figures like they're pieces of firewood. Dirt feasts on disfigured bodies that are nothing more than skin on bone.

"The dark continent," I mutter and run a hand along the top of her locker.

"What?" she asks.

"Is this it?" I ask.

"Thank God." She grabs the light from my hands. "I didn't know how I was going to explain it to my parents."

"Things disappear all the time."

"Like I said, you don't know Papa."

We walk back outside and she unlocks her bike then climbs on and puts her helmet on.

"Fabulous." I fiddle with the drawstring of Koech's hood.

"Right." She peddles away from me with her bike light securely attached to the handlebars.

Workout that evening is, according to Vivian, a real bitch. We run ten 800's with a two-minute recovery between each. Sam calls us together after we're finished.

"We all suffer the consequences when someone is late," he says. "Therefore, we must all share responsibility for it. I want everyone to sprint an extra series of five one-hundred-metre hills before we begin to warm down."

"Sam," I protest. "I wasn't late on purpose. I had a meeting with my English teacher. Then this girl lost her bike light, and I had to help her find it."

"Five hills. Or do you want everyone to do seven?"

I shut it.

"He's right," says Erica when we set out to do the first one. "You have your priorities all wrong. Stop talking and start doing."

I half-hope Kulvinder will jump in there and put up a spirited argument in my defense.

No such luck. He just looks soulfully at Erica and nods sagely.

"If it happens again," I murmur, "you can all take turns squirting Gatorade into my eyes."

Erica rolls her eyes and Kulvinder shoots me a sinister look.

"Odd fuck," Vivian giggles.

I'm shagged by the time I get home and I'm unprepared for what awaits me as I walk in the door.

Dad is yelling and pounding a fist on the kitchen table. "The big man has to go," he bellows. "There have been enough excuses. Moi has to go."

I peek my head in to see what's going on. He sits beside a pile of potato peels, the buttons of his shirt undone to his navel, while Mum bastes a chicken on the stove.

"Is everything okay?" I ask.

"Oh, John. Are you home?" Mum says. "We've just heard some terrible news. Terrible, terrible news."

My heart catches in my throat. "My God. What?"

"There's been bloodshed in the streets of Nairobi," Dad says. "We just heard it on BBC radio."

"The police broke up a prayer meeting by beating up university students," Mum adds.

I relax. For a moment I thought they'd heard something about Koech.

"People are suffering terribly because prices for the essentials are out of control," says Dad. "It's preposterous. Isn't this the sort of thing we kicked the *Wazungu* out over? I have half a mind to organize a protest. We can't just stand by while this sort of thing goes on. We have to let people here know what's happening."

"Ahab, don't get so worked up. We don't really know very much yet."

"It won't take much. We just have to print out some handbills and put them up around town. If we let people know, they'll turn out in droves."

Man, I really don't want to hear about it. I have two papers due, a presentation to make and a long run to get in over the weekend.

I take a bath and repose, like Caligula, in lukewarm water.

"You there." It's Dad, shouting in the kitchen. "I told you not to park in our spot." The front door slams against the wall. "Don't walk away from me. I'm talking to you."

I peek out the bathroom window: Dad and the *Wazungu* with the Fiat are nose to nose on the sidewalk.

"Take a chill pill, buddy." The *Wazungu* has a basketball tucked under one arm.

"I'm not your buddy."

"Freak."

Dad swats the ball out of the *Wazungu's* grasp. "Don't take me for a fool." He kicks it as hard as he can. The ball arches through the air and drops into the yard next door.

"Your Fiat will be next."

The *Wazungu* backs off. "You're whacko." He fumbles in his pockets for keys. "Whack-O."

"I'm not warning you again."

"If I can't find my ball, you'll pay for it."

Dad shoos him away.

I slide back into the tub as the Fiat rolls out of our spot. Lying there with my ears submerged under water.

Kulvinder pulls out a soccer ball and draws a chalk rectangle on the wall at the back end of their garden.

"We're going to Treetops next month," he says. "If you save this shot you can come with us."

"Treetops?"

"It's a hotel built in trees above a salty water hole that's surrounded by wild animals. Buffaloes. Elephants. Zebras. Baboons. We go there every year." He dribbles cautiously towards the net.

"All the guests are dropped off about one hundred yards from the hotel, and an armed escort of forest rangers has to walk you there. If not, you'll be attacked by animals close enough to spit on." I stare at him in disbelief. "I'm not making this up. It's the place Princess Elizabeth visited when she found out that her father, the King, was dead. That's how she became the Queen."

"Okay."

I crouch while he collects the ball on his instep and hesitates. I wait for his move.

He plows forward, lowers his head and spears me in the chest. When I come to, he's celebrating.

I'm woozy. "That doesn't count," I say.

"Sure it does."

"You fouled me."

"You fouled me," he whines. "Don't be such a cry baby."

"It doesn't count."

My heart presses against my lower rib.

"Cry baby." He sets up again in front of me.

I hold myself steady as best I can and stare him down.

He breaks hard towards the net. "Pele has the ball." He feints to the right, sits me on my buttocks and pulls to my left. "Pele shooooooooots!" He raises his arms in the air as the ball sails over my head and . . . over the wall into the slum behind us.

"You missed," I sneer.

"The ball!"

We aren't about to get it by ourselves. So I explain the problem to Koech.

"Let your ridiculous friend get it." He's busy with History homework.

"Pleeease."

"I have to finish this essay in a couple of hours if I'm going to get in an easy run before dark."

"Come on. I'll polish your boots."

He closes his textbook. "Forget the boots. You're coming for a run after you've finished your Math assignment."

"All right," I grumble.

"Good."

"Can I fetch the ball with you?" I want to go to the slum.

"John! Dad will skin you alive if you don't get any school work done before he gets home."

"Okay," I mutter.

Okay. I'll just wait till he's gone, then Kulvinder and I will follow after him.

Kulvinder disappears into his house. On his return he's carrying his Swiss Army knife.

"Cripes, Kulvinder!"

"It's for our protection," he replies.

"John," Mum shouts from the kitchen. "Telephone."

It's a little after nine. But I'm curled up in bed after a long soak in a hot tub of Epsom salts.

It's probably Kulvinder, apologizing for being such a moron at practice.

Sorry about that mate. Jugs is late again, and I think it might be for real this time. Protection! Who uses it these days? She says the pill brings on menopause and if I loved her . . .

"Hello."

"I got your number from Kulvinder."

"Svetlana!" There's a knock at the back door. "Listen, can I get you to hold a sec? There's someone at the door."

"Nahuh."

I open up and there's Slim.

"Leeds," he says. "Wanna see what I got?"

"Not if it's been dismembered in some way."

"Diswhat?"

"Cut open."

"Nooo," he laughs. "I got stitches. See." He lifts up a worn pant leg and points to a long gash across his shin.

Slim's a small kid for his age, and he's always getting into scraps.

"Maaan. How did that happen?"

"I got in a fight with Justin. We're not friends no more. He hit me with a hockey stick, and that's why I got stitches." He pulls a baseball bat from behind his back. "But I'm gonna fix him. I'm gonna bust up that pussy punk bitch."

I'm too tired to deal with his crap. "Listen, I've got someone on the phone."

"Is it your old lady?"

"I don't have an old lady."

"I bet it is. Is she stacked?"

"Keep it down, man. She'll hear you."

But he's already slipped past me and picked up the phone. "Who is this? Svetlana!! Ooooooo. Are you his old lady or what? Uhuh. I have one too. No. Nooooo. She's gonna give me twelve children. How many children you gonna give Leeds? Hold up. Hold up."

I tug on the receiver. "Don't be a pest."

"Sucker." He lets go and splits to fill Jugs in on these latest developments.

"Sorry about that," I say to Svetlana. "It's just—"

"No need to explain. He's adorable."

"He's a royal pain is what he is." There is silence.

Then, "How about getting together to, uh, discuss our project?" she says.

Slim left the front door wide open. When I go to shut it, I notice Dad dragging a huge cement block from the yard.

"What are you doing?" I ask.

"Good, John. Give us a hand."

Out on the street three blocks have been placed in our empty parking spot.

"One more should do it," he says.

We walk over to a pile of rubble and grab another block, which we carry out to the street.

"Do you think we ought to be doing this?" I ask.

"That fellow is a typical *Wazungu*." He bends to adjust the final brick. "No respect. I've talked to him several times, but he continues to park here."

I fidget with the zipper of Koech's sweat top. "I should probably get back inside. I have homework."

"Son, I've been thinking about the protest. I'd like to get as many people out as we can and see what sort of pressure we can put on the Canadian government to intervene. Do you think you could help me with the handbills on Saturday afternoon?"

"You're kidding."

"Not at all."

"Come on, Dad. I've got track practice."

"What do you mean, come on? There are surely more important things in the world than practice."

"Dad."

"When I was your age, I worked tirelessly to see that the *Wazungu* left the country. We had no idea how it would happen. But we did what we could. I had this good friend. A Luo fellow named Okot. His brother was killed when Harry Thuku was thrown in jail. You don't remember Thuku, do you? Probably not, you know all about Henry the Eighth and the Pilgrims, but you know nothing of your own history. Well, Okot's brother joined a crowd of protesters outside the jail. There were thousands of them, shouting and singing and demanding that he be released. That was when the police panicked. They fired into the crowd, even though some of the protesters held up a white flag. Do you think this stopped them? Not a chance. They kept on shooting, and his brother was killed."

"I'm not missing practice."

"You really haven't a clue. I saw them kill Okot. The security forces came to our high school looking for members of the *Mau Mau*. Can you imagine that? They were young, still only boys. And they made a group of us crouch down on our haunches. Then, one by one, they stripped us down, asked us to give them our names and whipped us with a *kiboko*. Okot tried to escape by jumping out a window, and he was dead by the—"

"—time his body hit the ground."

"You understand nothing. Nothing about what we fought for and even less about what is left to achieve. Just look at how this *Wazungu* with the Fiat treats us."

"Dad, these things happened years ago."

"John, I'm not asking you. I'm telling you. You're going to help me give out handbills."

Not if I can help it. I'm uncomfortable enough about the bricks in the parking spot. He can drive a spit through me and roast me over a flame if that's what it comes to. I still won't have anything to do with his stupid rally.

"You didn't help Koech with his protest," I smirk.

He stiffens.

I stomp off to my bedroom and lock the door.

"John, get back here. John!"

It feels fantastic for about a minute and a half. Then I'm scared shitless. Especially when he bangs on the door.

I flip up Koech's hood, tighten the drawstring and wait for Mum to drag him away.

Mum, Dad, Koech and I sit down to supper.

Quietly we peck away at our ugali and sukumawiki with nyama.

Dad's all cockeyed because of problems at work. Mum's mind is buzzing from a busy day of teaching, and Koech ponders whether or not to rat me out.

"I was in the slum today," Koech blurts. "No one should have to live like that."

Mum reaches over to smooth the sleeve of Dad's jacket. "It's been drier than most seasons, Son, so people are moving from rural areas into the city looking for jobs. It's unfortunate, but this is just what happens."

"Something has to be done," Koech replies.

"We've lobbied Mutui at city council to have the damn thing levelled," Dad says.

"Levelled!" It's Mum. "But they'll have nowhere to go."

I don't care much for the subject. Koech might just open his big gob.

"Dad!"

Even if he does keep the afternoon a secret, I still have to head him off before they enter one of those conversations that leave them quieter, more severe.

"Dad!"

"Don't talk with your mouth full," Dad snaps.

I swallow a morsel of ugali. "Have you heard of Treetops?"

"If anyone touches the slum, I'll organize a protest," Koech interrupts.

"Oh, Koech," Dad replies. "Don't you have enough to worry about, balancing your running with school?"

"I'll make time."

"Son, these matters are far too complicated for you to understand," Dad says. "It's business, that's all. The Weaver Consortium has put in a considerable bid to develop the land which, in turn, will create both capital and jobs. This is a good thing."

"I thought you were a socialist."

"Were, past tense." Dad laughs. "We all have periods of idealism."

"Don't you care about people anymore?"

"Of course I care," Dad replies. "But globalization and freer international markets mean biting the bullet. Eventually these matters correct themselves."

"That sounds awful."

"Don't be naive," Dad snaps. "I haven't seen you forsake any of the comforts foreign investments help us purchase."

"Koech has a point," Mum says. "Sometimes the price paid for that investment is just too high."

"Not you as well, Gladys," Dad replies.

"Kulvinder invited me to Treetops," I interrupt.

Koech glares at me.

"Can I go?"

They ignore me. Everyone gets quiet again.

OCTOBER:
The Outer Lane

1

Erica, Kulvinder and I stretch in goose turds after practice as we wait for Vivian and Sam to return from a long walk.

"They've been gone a while," I say. "I wonder what that's about?"

In any other circumstance Kulvinder would start squeezing imaginary titties and making loud humping noises, but not in front of Erica. "I hope it's nothing too serious," he says.

"She's got problems with the law."

"Shut up!" I exclaim.

"It's true. She has some sort of probation order that says she has to return to her group home after every practice."

"That's an awful lot for her to go through right now." More horse wallop I've never heard come out Kulvinder's mouth before.

"It's not the sort of thing that she wants people to know about her."

He looks at her with doe-eyed concern. "We won't tell a soul. Not a word."

"Sam is working at having it taken care of. He met with her case worker and probation officer to discuss things this morning. But any change is dependent on a court appearance in the middle of November."

"What did she do, steal a car?" I ask.

"That's inappropriate, Leeds. Erica has told us more than we need to know."

His tone is calm and measured. It's enough to make me puke.

"No. It's okay," she says. "It's probably better that you know. She stabbed a worker at one of her placements with a bread knife. Stuck her right in the arm because she went into her bedroom without permission."

"Wow," I say. "She's nice enough for an arm-stabber. She doesn't seem to have much of a temper or anything."

Kulvinder stares off into nothingness. Then he comes out with, "The wind is struggling in her sleep, comfortless because she is a giant."

"God, Kulvinder," Erica says. "That is so beautiful."

It was. But it isn't his. He lifted the quote from a poem.

Damn, I wish I'd come up with it first, anything to wedge a gap between them.

Those two have been involved in a subtle form of foreplay since Sam punished everyone with extra hills the day I was late. They burst into giggles, whisper often and exchange knowing looks.

Then, for consummation, they use workouts to collectively kick me in the tush.

I lie in bed the following night and work on the splits it will take to break 1.50.

If I take the first 200 out in twenty-seven, I can run fairly even twos. This means going through the four in fifty-four. It's quick. But I just have to stay relaxed. The third two's the fucker. I can't afford to lose focus. Turn my legs over and save enough for one last push off the final bend. Cruz usually makes a break with 350 to go. But that seems too early, unless I practice long runs home during workouts. Just press from way out and run through. Press and run. Just press and run . . .

Aluminum dustbins clattering against one another in the back alley interrupt me.

I peek out the window.

Jugs and Slim stagger under the weight of their mother. Her knees buckle above her dragging feet.

I slip on a pair of sweats, rush outside and find them collapsed next to a pile of rusty metal.

"C'mon, Ma," Slim says, getting to his feet. "It ain't far."

Her dress is hiked up around her waist, and she's not wearing underwear.

"Here," I tug on her arm.

"Sonoffabitch," she murmurs. "Fugginsonoffabitch."

"Get the door, Slim," Jugs says. "We'll get her inside."

He races off as we lift the missus, place her arms over our shoulders, smooth down her dress and help her towards her suite.

"Slim, you'll have to give us a hand," I say when we reach the back stairs. "Put your arm around her waist and keep her steady."

We struggle up a flight of bannisterless stairs, drag her through the kitchen and plop her down on a couch covered in laundry. "Where's Larry?" I ask.

"I say, where ya goin?" Slim replies. "He says to get a paper."

"He lef is what," the missus says. "Took off. Yesserday. Jus like that. The sonofabitch. An he ain't never comin back."

"We're better off without him, Ma."

"Don't say that, Steph," Slim says. "He's gonna come back."

The missus continues to mutter, a lazy dribble of spittle making its way down her pale chin.

"Slim, get my mum. She'll know what to do."

Slim hurries off, and I watch Jugs prop her mum's head up with a pillow.

Mum and Dad carry the missus into the bathroom.

"We'll have to keep her awake with a cold shower," Mum says. "Stephanie, make up a pot of strong coffee."

"John, take the boy downstairs," Dad adds.

It's the first time he's said boo to me since our fallout.

Slim and I sit at the kitchen table. His feet swing rapidly under his chair. "Want some milk?" I ask.

"I'm allergic."

"Something else then?"

"Coke."

"How 'bout orange juice?"

"Bleckh."

"Coke it is then."

Repeatedly, the back of Slim's heel bangs the leg of his chair.

"Ma's gonna be okay. Right, Leeds?"

"Right." I hand it to him. "She's just a little sad. But she'll be okay."

"When Larry gets back he'll fix everything up. Right, Leeds?"

"Course he will. But for now you need to get some sleep."

He slurps down the Coke and burps. Then I lead him to my room and give him Koech's sweat top to sleep in. I wait outside while he changes.

"Ready?" I shout after a couple of minutes.

"Yep."

"Okay." I let myself back in. "Use the bathroom. Then it's time to get to bed." It's 2:45. I have to be up for a morning run at six. "Hey, where the hell are you going?" He's already making his way out of the bathroom. "You wash up?"

"Uhuh."

"Bathroom," I say. "Here's a towel for you to wipe up with. Now wash those hands and that mucky face of yours." He splashes water onto his hands. "That isn't a wash." I take the bar of soap and scrub his hands and face for him. He laughs and bends his neck towards the sink as I splash it with water. "Hands." He rinses them and dries off with a towel. "Now for your teeth." I give him a spare toothbrush he slops paste all over. "Get those back teeth. And don't forget to get in a good gargle. Excellent. Now, you're ready for bed."

He hurries under the covers and I pull sheets up to his chin. "Member Justin?"

"Yeh."

"I fixed 'im up good with the bat."

"Goodnight, Slim."

"G'night."

I pull a sleeping bag out from the closet and set it up on the floor beside the door. But by the time I turn the lights off, he's already asleep.

Sounds drift over the wall, different than the ones before; rattling joints, fingernails that scratch the soil, racks of rib cages banging pelvic bones. They rise from the flattened cardboard and gather at the wall. Crinkled feet mounting spines that splinter. Fingertips stretched towards barbed wire. The smell creeping in through the window. Natives. An eruption of voices stirs the rotten, motionless air. Languages I don't understand. Crackling charcoal. Brown cheeks like mine . . .

I want to help them.

I'm afraid of them.

I wish they'd just be quiet.

I wake with a start, dress and head outside.

On the front stair Jugs sits biting her bottom lip.

I squish down beside her, put my arm around her and wait.

"Leeds," says Jugs. "I was thinking of having a party. I'd invite some people. You could bring, like, your track friend. What's her name, Erica. Kulvinder says she's nice."

I don't say anything.

"I'll ask Svetlana to come?" she continues.

I want to tell her about the nightmare. "Want to know something?"

She starts examining her nails. "Uhuh." Then she dabs at her rouged cheeks with a brush.

"Never mind."

Svetlana and I sit at the fifty-yard line of the soccer pitch. She's working on a salad in a plastic container. I munch on an orange peel.

The night's activities gave us some things to talk about. But we'd about chewed the hell out of that topic.

We segue into the obligatory revelations. She was born in a small town near an unpronounceable city in Siberia. Krasnoyarsk or something. Her old man used to be a chauffeur for a government official, while her old lady worked in a plant that produced uranium used in nuclear missiles. When the Soviet Union started going belly up in the mid-eighties, they both lost their jobs. Svetlana was four when they moved to Vancouver. Now her old man is a mechanic, and the old lady is a maid. I tell her my dad's on the dole and my mum is a social worker. I don't want to get into much more.

"Any thoughts on the project?" Svetlana finally asks.

"Huh?"

"I figured we should do something that'll blow people's socks off, like guerrilla theatre. Something that messes with their ideas about what's theatrical and what's real." I stare at her. "We wouldn't have a stage. We'd just roam between desks . . ." I focus on a gap between her front teeth, gaze at lips broken into flaking ridges. ". . . Then we'd do some dancing, body contact dancing. You know, rolling on the floor in all sorts of contorted positions. Playing out that scene where Othello murders Desdemona."

"That sounds . . ." I can't take any of it in.

"Flicking cool."

"Yes."

"Finch'll flip."

"Yes."

I don't have the balls to skip practice that evening. So I do my best despite a lack of sleep.

By the time we run the second of our six 1200's, I'm fucked.

I approach Sam as if I'd been entrusted to take his car out for a spin and smashed it into a lamp post. "I don't think I can go on. I had a rough night at home and . . ."

He sighs melodramatically. "You're full of excuses, you know that?"

"It isn't like that. The woman who lives . . ."

"Leeds is quitting on us, folks."

I stare at the ground.

"It ain't his fault," Vivian mumbles.

"You quitting on us too?" Sam searches his pockets for cigarettes. Then gives up with a grunt. "All right. Enough nattering. Time for the next one."

I can't make sense of how I'm supposed to act anymore. "She was drunk . . ."

"I'd like this next one to be closer to eighty percent."

"Fuck, Sam." I'm losing it. "I'm trying to explain."

He stands there waiting for everyone to line up.

The bastard isn't going to ignore me.

I rush at him, my arms flailing.

He picks them easily out of the air, flips me on my back and sits on me.

"Fuck you, asshole. Fuck off. Fuck you." I wriggle and scream beneath him. "Dickhead." Struggling against his weight until I'm spent.

He waits a moment. Then lifts me to my feet. "Time for the next one."

I should collapse at his feet and refuse to budge. But my reasons for doing so suddenly seem ridiculous. Sure I'm buggered. But Cruz would dig down and pull another interval out of his ass.

Reluctantly I line up with the others. Erica drops her hand, and we're away.

It's as if a needle has been shoved into the base of my spine; pain radiating in ripples through my bone marrow.

The agony isn't strictly physical, though. It's in my head, the message finally getting through. I'm no Koech. No matter how much I try, I'll never be good enough.

After practice I lie down away from everyone. I put Koech's hood up and sob until my stomach cramps. I can't stop, and wish Sam would come over and tell me I'm going to be okay. He waits till the others have warmed down, gets in his car and drives home.

When I get back to my place I head straight for my room.

A stack of guides and application forms to universities lies beside the bed. I kick them across the room, clamber under the covers and fall asleep with the light on.

A little after three, I wake up. I climb out of bed, go to the bathroom and slice myself for the first time in a while.

Blood oozes from my arms, but my mind won't stop churning.

I meet Koech in the front yard.

"Pour soi," Koech says.

"What are you on about now?" I ask.

"Jean-Paul Sartre, a French bloke, said personal existence is about being aware. We're free to choose, and in doing so we accept the consequences of our actions."

"I don't understand," I reply.

"You will," he says.

I run through a one-hundred-metre obstacle course. I'm dipping, leaping and crawling to the finish.

"You can do better than that," Koech announces.

I jog back to the start and go again. This time I thrash my arms and plow towards each obstacle with abandon.

"Your form is terrible, Leeds," Koech comments. "Here." He pushes the top of my forehead. "Keep your head up and don't drop your shoulders." He taps me on the solar plexus. "Take deeper breaths." He demonstrates. "It'll help you to recover."

After ten minutes I'm knackered and plunk down on the grass at Koech's feet.

"Get up," he says. "Walk it off."

If I wasn't so dizzy I'd scratch his eyes out.

Koech puts me in a headlock. "Airs of superiority are a product of lazy thinking. They hide weaknesses rather than build strength. Do you follow?"

"Yeh." I kick the grass beneath his feet.

"Good," he responds. "You have five minutes before we start the next set."

"Another one!" I exclaim.

Koech slaps my bum.

"Heifer lump. What did you do, swallow a bunch of shit balls?" He fancies I need to go on a diet. "Yeh, one more set."

I touch my buttocks and notice how they've gone out of their way. Bulky. Round. Horrible.

I do rolls and sprints. Push-ups. Sit-ups. Rolls and sprints again. I scrape up my knees and get grass in my teeth.

3

The following morning Kulvinder tries to help put the shabby practice behind me. He suggests that a good wank and an evening out is all I need.

"Here's some free advice," he says. "Never underestimate the potential of tying one on. It gets the blood pumping to your extremities and puts the jump back in your step. Both Steph and Svetlana are game. I'm not taking no for an answer, and don't even think about thanking me. I'm just happy knowing I can be of some help. You'll be there for someone else I'm sure."

I should offer up my confession right away, how I carry a torch for Jugs. Let him know how uncomfortable it will be doubling with Svetlana.

Instead, there I sit, later that night, living it up with his assembled crew.

We crowd into a sandbox, stare at dots of yellow light glowing from the Science World dome and pass around wine coolers. Everything begins to loosen up as we guzzle the fizzy sweetness.

Svetlana has cut her hair into one of those Hamlet dos. Short at the ear and slightly longer at the back. There's a hint of blush on her cheeks; her lips are bright red and she wears eyeliner. It's the first time I've seen her in makeup, and she looks pretty good.

Kulvinder is his usual charming self. He elaborates on our naughty days. The odd kicked-in bank machine or mangled public telephone. All of this told with pauses I fill with my own embellishments.

Somewhere in all that fuzziness Jugs and Kulvinder start jawing at each other.

"It don't make no sense," Jugs says. "If Erica don't mean nothing, then why can't I meet her?"

"You're embarrassing yourself."

"I know you're fucking her. You're fucking her. Aren't you?"

Kulvinder grabs hold of her wrist and twists. "Show some class, damnit."

Svetlana tackles him by the legs, and I put a hand on his shoulder.

"Chill, Kulvinder." I'm shocked by his outburst. "Chill."

"Stay out of this." He shrugs us both off.

"I'm sorry," Jugs whimpers.

He lets go. "Don't be a bitch your whole life," he says.

"But I love you."

"Christ, we're out here to show my friend a good time, and this is what I get."

"I didn't mean nothing." Her fingers root through the stubble at his chin. Her head tips forward to nuzzle his cheek. "I really love you." Her mouth arranges itself into a depression at his temple, conversation between them breath and murmurs.

I look at Svetlana. "Let's get out of here."

We brush ourselves off and go sit on a pair of swings.

"That was unpleasant," I say.

"Unpleasant!" She's upset. "She needs to file a report with the police."

"I'll talk to him."

"Damn right you better talk to him. He needs treatment before Steph ends up in a battered women's shelter."

"I will." She's overreacting. "I swear."

We stare at the sand beneath us, and I wait for her to calm down, then I start to jabber off the top of my head. "Sex just complicates relationships. People ought to spend more time getting to know one another."

"No argument here," she replies.

I dig my heels into the ground and lift a sleeve. The fresh cuts are near my wrist.

"Does it hurt?" she asks.

"Not really."

"How long . . ."

"A year or so."

My heart pounds as she runs her fingers over each wrist.

"I'm not into assletes you know," she murmurs.

"Neither am I."

My lips quiver when I kiss her throat.

"These damn mosquitoes are driving me crazy," I hear Kulvinder complain.

"We oughta go back to my place," Jugs replies. "Mum 'n Slim are staying with a friend tonight."

"You guys want to go?" I hear Kulvinder ask.

Svetlana and I beat a hasty retreat back to the sandbox.

"I'll take that as a yes," Kulvinder says.

It will take some cunning to sneak into the back without being detected by the folks.

I'm anxious. Not so much about getting busted, but more because I've never been with a chick with such balls. I'll just stay with saliva-free kisses and leave all the decisions to her.

We creep around rusty automotive parts on our way to the back stairs.

"I'll go first," Jugs whispers.

She climbs up to the second floor, unlocks the door and signals for us to follow.

We crouch, a crack squad of patriotic oafs stalking Iraqis in the Gulf. Then we bolt.

I'm halfway up the stairs when Mum pops her head out a window. "Hold on, kids. Mrs. Bates has a message for Stephanie." Then she disappears inside leaving us standing on the stairs.

"Quick. Svetlana, your sweater." Kulvinder grabs it from her and wraps it around the box of coolers.

I want to make a run for it. Svetlana pulls on her bangs, and Kulvinder tucks the bigass bundle under his arm. Then Mum appears on the back porch, a piece of paper in her hand. "Here, give this to Stephanie, will you?" She hands it to Kulvinder.

"Sure, Mrs. Kipligat."

"Don't stay up too late," she adds, grinning.

"No problem, Mum."

As soon as she turns to go, Kulvinder loses his grip on the box. Bottles tumble out and shatter all over the stairs.

Mum looks at me as though she's been ambushed from all angles.

"I'd like Kulvinder and Svetlana to go home."

She could cut diamonds with her look.

4

Kulvinder and I aren't allowed to go to track anymore. We're under house arrest. The only time we can venture out is to go either to work or to school.

Dad grunts at me even less than before, and Mum has taken to giving me an I'm-so-disappointed look every time I see her.

Why's it such a big fucking deal? We didn't smoke crack. We only drank a couple of coolers, for Christ sake.

Anyway, I couldn't give a shit. Sam has entered us in an indoor meet in Calgary next month. "If you want to get the attention of American scouts, you'll have to run some respectable times early," he said. "They have so much talent down south that you'll have to make them come to you. But don't worry about it too much. You should be able to step onto the track at any time of the year and run within five percent of your optimum performance."

It's all too rich for me. I'll only succeed in making a fool of myself.

As far as I'm concerned, the folks can ground me for as long as they want.

My drunken night out creates weird tension between Mum and Dad.

His first inquiry on getting home late from a collectively run cafe he's begun spending time in is, "Your mother in?"

"Not yet," I reply.

He relaxes, helps himself to whatever food she's left in the oven and buries himself in the living room under a pile of leftist magazines.

When Mum returns from work, she heads for a long bath. Her brief comments to Dad are filled with jibes. "I see you subscribed to the *Utne Reader*. We still haven't paid the hydro bill, and you've subscribed to yet another magazine." Or, "The cafe. Don't you think it might be more productive spending that time at the unemployment office?"

Then she retires to hunch down at her altar and read configurations in her pebbles.

Thank God, family day is history. But I still find it stressful to be anywhere near them. Especially when they get wind of even more gossip about my derelict ways.

Chan Lu, one of the hookers, casually drops to Mum that I offered her cigarettes in exchange for a blow job. A complete fabrication. I only asked the question in the abstract. However, the impact was major since her comments came on the heels of a chat they requested with Principal Hammond.

A family meeting is called, and the television is turned off. Dad begins. "We met with Principal Hammond to find out how you've been doing at school. God knows it's impossible to get a straight answer out of you."

"He says your grades have dropped to D's."

Mum hands me pamphlets. They discuss depression, anger management, alcoholism and substance abuse. "He thinks you should meet with the school counsellor. But your father's dead set against it."

"The counsellor will blame us for everything," Dad says. "That's all people do in this country. Lay blame. He didn't get enough attention from his parents. He wasn't nurtured enough in his formative years. Well, that's because the parents were too busy putting food into the ungrateful bugger's mouth."

I'm weary. "I'm not an alcoholic," I reply.

They've already moved on. "I always felt Kulvinder was a bad influence," Dad continues. "Koech always managed to balance school work with his athletics, but you aren't coping."

"We've tried everything with you, John." Mum's cheek twitches. "But you've taken advantage, and it has to stop. I can't stay up nights worrying that you'll end up in jail. It's not fair to either one of us. From now on you'll spend the time you went to track practice at work with me. I don't care if this upsets you. It'll do you good to be around people with real problems."

They might as well have pushed me under the back wheels of a truck.

Dad's brow cracks into ridges. "You spent the whole day with the Indian boy, didn't you."

I shrug.

"I've warned you about neglecting your studies, John," Dad says.

"Sod off," I shout.

"What did you say?"

"I'll spend time with Kulvinder if I want to."

Dad stands up, disappears into his study and returns with a ruler. "Put your hand out," he says.

The first blow stings.

I purse my lips.

Dad's eyes are bright with light and he wallops my knuckles for the fourth time.

I try to out-stare him, but by the sixth stroke, I can't hold back. Tears burst out like water from a fire hydrant.

Svetlana is allowed to stop by to prepare for our presentation, and she charms the folks with talk about the necessity of international banks forgiving debt in the developing world.

When we retire to my bedroom, she pushes the furniture against the walls then lights long red candles before putting spacey, atmospheric slop in the cassette deck.

We sit beside one another on my lumpy mattress. "Are we going to have to wear veils?" I ask.

"See-through veils," she replies. "Great idea."

"I'm not serious."

She ignores me. "Costumes will come later. Right now we should concentrate on the performance."

"Well, this music you've chosen is crap," I say.

"It's late Miles Davis."

"Sorry, I should have said pretentious crap."

"Don't you listen to jazz?"

"Why?" I snap. "Because I'm black?"

"No." She takes a breath. "I didn't mean it like that."

I ease off. "Gimme a drum machine and I'll pop'n lock all over the dance floor. This shite is bizarre."

"It's all about finding the language in his music." She takes my hand. "Don't think. Just trust your impulses. Mood can be radically changed by the subtlest vibration."

Before I have a chance to orient myself, she's lying on top of me, and we're rolling together across the floor.

"Always maintain body contact." She stands and pulls me onto my feet between her legs. Then turns me so we're butt cheek to butt cheek and rolling our hips.

Afterwards we hold hands on the window ledge and look out into the alleyway, where we watch Johns make drop-offs and pick-ups.

"Where did you learn to dance like that?" I ask.

"It's one of the improv exercises we use to warm up in acting class."

"You never mentioned you were an actress."

Her face flushes. "I've still got a long way to go before I'm ready to study at the National Theatre in Moscow."

"Cool," I say.

"My parents don't like it, though. They want me to be an engineer. That's what Papa always wanted to do. They've got it in their heads that we'll go back to Siberia some day, and I'll use my education to make us rich."

"Fuck that."

"I understand where they're coming from. People think Siberia is just a barren place where Stalin sent prisoners to die in concentration camps. But it's more than that. The land has the largest gas reserves in the world."

"Hell, let somebody else exploit it; you're an actress."

We gossip.

"Finch's been hitting on girls in the Condoms In Bathrooms Committee," she says.

"Not true."

"Why not? Teachers and students have affairs all the time."

"Not him." I laugh. "Mrs. Finch is scrogged up with their second child."

"Wake up, Leeds," she snipes. "Finch'd rather have improprieties with teenage girls than commit to an adult relationship with his wife."

"That's nuts."

"You're such a flicking guy sometimes." She reaches into her backpack. "You and Kulvinder both." She pulls out a cellophane bag and chews a celery stick. "Have you talked to him yet?"

"Yeh," I lie. "He doesn't mean to lose it. He's just all stirred up inside like that artist that chopped off his ear. Van Gogh."

She snorts. "Tell me you're kidding."

"Anyway, he promised never to do it again," I reply.

I switch gears and gab about Koech.

"I have an older brother, you know."

"Really."

"He's a runner, a great runner. When he was sixteen he ran 1.46 in the 800, and if he hadn't been injured that year, he'd have broken the four-minute mile."

"Does he live in Kenya?"

"I don't know."

"What do you mean, you don't know?"

"He disappeared."

"Oh, God. I'm sorry."

She touches my hand and I flinch.

"I don't want to make a big deal about it. Okay?"

"Okay."

Koech preps to run the senior boys' 800 metres. He's isolated himself in the infield of the 400-metre grass oval. The hood of his blue track top up, his legs splayed out on either side of him as he stretches his groin muscles.

Koech flops onto his back, then shakes his limbs.

"Runners to the start," the starter yells.

He strips down to a bright yellow singlet and shorts, a light sweat burnishing his muscles as he strolls onto the track.

A field of ten settles into place.

"On your mark."

Koech darts forward in lane one, plants his right foot behind the chalk start line and hunches over.

BANG.

He gets out in a hurry, and no one is within ten metres of him when he enters the second bend. Is he light on his feet? No question about it. He has long, lanky legs that go right up into his buttocks, and when he runs, he lopes. Real classy. Just skimming along the grass surface like a hovercraft. Whoosh. Whoosh.

"22, 23, 24."

His split at the two is twenty-three seconds; excited students crowd the track to watch.

"Go Koech," I scream.

He cruises clean through the turn and doesn't let up on the straightaway, his head dead still, like he's balancing a clay water pot.

"48, 49, 50."

He's reached the quarter in forty-nine seconds. If he keeps this up, he'll drop kick the high school record into a crater in Mount Longanot.

I'm giddy.

His legs gobble the bend before he shifts into a relaxed canter with three to go.

Kathunk. Kathunk. Kathunk.

When he pulls into the final stretch, over one hundred metres clear of the field, my chest tightens. The ease with which he's destroying the competition tickles my ribs.

"1.45, 1.46, 1.47."

He's run 1.46.3 and shattered the standard.

5

Butting heads with Mum and Dad isn't going to get me out of this jam. I'll have to weasel my way back into their good graces by buttering their toast.

I decide to work them separately.

Dad's arranged a meeting at the house with some open-sandalled types he met at his favourite cafe on Commercial Drive. So I let him know how eager I am to sit in and take notes.

They all have a zillion and one ideas. Striking up search committees. Opening an office. Petitions. Telephone trees. Building a black community centre. All of these ideas thrown out between stories about having it stuck to them by the man.

Somewhere in there a tentative date is set for a rally in front of the art gallery steps.

It's enough to drive me round the bend. But I nod, cluck at appropriate times and pledge my troth.

Mum is a tougher nut to crack. She's stressed from working double shifts.

My solution is to get domestic. Ironing. Cooking meals. Watering plants. Pitching in with the groceries. The works.

Even I'm smitten with myself.

Unfortunately it doesn't wash.

So I pull out the heavy artillery and come up with a way to show her how my stint at her job is having an effect.

I'll take the two-hour bus ride after school and donate some Spiderman comics to Daniel, the kid she cares for. It's perfect. Thoughtful and considerate without involving money.

I steady myself with a quick hit of fresh air, open the front door and make straight for his bedroom.

Mum's busy trying to make Daniel comfortable in his bed. "Calf." She scratches an itch on his flaking, sallow skin. "Higher." She makes the adjustment. "Lower." She tries again. "NO, NO. You're doing it all wrong. I said calf."

"I'm just following your instructions."

"HIGHER. Are you stupid? HIGHER."

The kid is fourteen going on eighty-three. His mind is as keen as a brand new machete, while his bloated, dwarfish body gives out, organ by organ and limb by limb.

His health has declined to the point where he's dependent on others for everything. A cup with a straw has to be lifted to his lips whenever he barks, "Drink." Smushed food is spooned into the side of his drooping mouth at meal times, and pages are turned for him whenever he emerges from an overdose of the telly.

"Mum, I was rummaging through some old magazines and thought Daniel might like these comics."

"Put them on the dresser."

"Hey, Daniel. How are you doing?"

He ignores me. "I need the toilet. Where's Hilaal? HILAAL."

I step aside and a frail Eritrean woman pops into the room. "I am right here, Daniel."

She's a refugee who narrowly escaped jail by lugging her child through the desert and into a crowded Red Cross camp in Northern Kenya.

Hilaal turns a lever and raises the back of Daniel's bed. Meanwhile, Mum sets up a contraption with a hanging harness that dangles about four feet off the ground.

"Ow." They gently manoeuvre Daniel to the edge of the bed. "My back. WATCH MY BACK." Each of them takes a leg under one arm and supports his back with the other. "Be careful." His face scrunches up. "Hurry. HURRY. I have to go."

As soon as they manage to secure him in the harness, he does indeed go. No time for anyone to get a bucket under him, just a stream of diarrhea that splatters all over their shoes.

"Look what you did. Idiots."

Man, I know the kid won't live long enough to experience the joys of a steamy snog, but he's an asshole to Mum.

On Wednesday morning the following week, Svetlana and I huddle on the front steps at school.

She's trembling and upset. "I still can't believe it." Finch has been canned.

"There's got to be some mistake." I don't know what else to say.

"No. Stephanie wouldn't make up a thing like that." He supposedly asked her to tame his wily tallywacker. "It all makes me feel kind of weird."

"Weirder than usual."

"I'm serious. He said he liked my work. But he could have been saying that to get in my pants."

"Don't talk rubbish. Finch wasn't like that. Stephanie probably led him on."

She pulls away and scrunches her face. "You're a callow prick."

"Whatever," I say. "Anyway, his loss is our gain. We won't have to go through with that mad presentation anymore."

She tugs the straps of her knapsack over both shoulders. "You know what, don't flicking call me anymore."

I find Kulvinder comforting Jugs in the hallway. They're pressed up against a locker. "We won't let the fucker get away with it, baby." His eyes are red with rage.

"Don't do anything crazy, sweetie," she pleads.

"Maybe you should listen to Stephanie," I add.

Two kids walk by, and one of them looks our way.

"What did you say?" Kulvinder asks him.

"Nothing," the skinny one with large ears replies.

"Don't say nothing," Kulvinder shouts. "If you've got something to say, let's hear it."

"It's nothing, Kulvinder," I whisper. He's drawing a crowd.

"Nothing, huh?" Kulvinder claps the kid across the head then doubles him over with a succession of punches to the stomach.

I jump in and wrap my arms around Kulvinder.

"Take me home, sweetie," Jugs sobs.

Kulvinder pushes me hard against the locker. Raises his fists and lunges at me.

When I flinch, he sneers before turning to give the kid one more kick for good measure.

Jugs falls into his arms. "Please, baby, get me outta here."

"All right, luv."

I help the kid to his feet and buy his silence with the promise of jujubes and a pack of Juicy Fruit.

After school I camp out beside Svetlana's bicycle until she shows up.

"Here." I hand her a letter. "Read it." She crumples it up and throws it on the ground. Then she unlocks her bike.

I scramble to pick it up and begin to read. "I'm sorry. I shouldn't have said what I did." She climbs on her bike and begins to pedal. I chase after her, skip forward to page four. "I haven't cut myself since we got together. I've wanted to. But you give me a reason to quit." She stops and I paraphrase the rest. "I'm making an effort. I've never done that before."

She takes the letter from my hand, and we french in the parking lot for a while.

Over the next couple of days life at home gets worse. Mum and Dad bicker in ways I've never seen before.

"Did you get your resume in at the bookstore?" Mum asks.

"Do I ask whether you get to work on time?" he replies.

"I expressly stated 'pick up some carrots,'" Mum says. "We need carrots."

Dad flings open a fridge stuffed with produce. "She has everything she needs, and she's going on about the carrots."

I begin to think divorce. Mine from them.

On the second night I get out of bed for a quick wizz. I can hear them whispering.

"Don't you think I've tried with John?" Dad says.

"He needs a father not a politician."

"You still blame me for Koech, don't you? That's what this is about." Something crashes against the wall. "It wasn't my fault."

"I never said it was."

"You don't have to, Gladys," Dad replies.

I sink down to the floor, everything dropping into darkness around me.

Koech sits in front of a mirror in his bedroom and sobs.

"Are you okay?" I ask.

"Go away," he replies.

I place my hand on his forearm and he stiffens, his skin drawing tight around the hard muscles. He gazes at his reflection, and I wonder what has upset him.

"Go away," he repeats.

I leave.

Dad's weekend rally is a bust.

His fellow protesters find one reason or another not to show; last-minute shifts at work, pressing ball games to go to and dental hygienists to fondle. The Kipligat family is left standing like clods in front of four bike couriers on a lunch break.

Dad is sullen.

He stops reading his magazines and upgrades the number of times he checks to see if the *Wazungu* with the Fiat has moved the cement blocks.

Mum, on the other hand, throws herself into non-stop rounds of domestic chores whenever she has time off work. Or she kneels before her altar and invokes the spirit of the Knowledge Holders, whom she asks for guidance.

Both of them treat me like a jailbird out on parole. They routinely rummage through my dresser drawers, where they expect to find contraband, and they carefully monitor my phone calls. They even go through a transparent charade of doing a breath check whenever I walk in the door.

I resent it. Tiptoeing through the house, tension in my belly, isn't how I intend to spend the rest of the year.

I look forward to Svetlana's visits. She needs a hand to prepare three audition pieces for a show at the Arts Club, and I read dialogue with her. On occasion I provide feedback about her monologues. Stuff like, I don't get what the character is feeling here, or, that line should be, uh, punched out more. I'm out of my element, but she's grateful.

Afterwards I bitch about how unhappy I am, but she takes it the wrong way and worries that I'll cut myself again.

"I figured it out," she says. "If you do two back-to-back laps in fifty-three seconds, you'll run 1.46 in the eight."

"It's not that simple."

"Why not?" she replies.

"That's like me saying, if you imitate Meryl Streep's performance in *Sophie's Choice*, you'll become a tip-top actress."

"You never know until you try."

"Trying is overrated," I say. "Making an effort has never made an ounce of difference in my life."

Her voice rises. "It doesn't always have to be that way."

"Jesus," I reply. "Don't get your knickers in a knot."

"Who knows what would've happened to us if my parents

hadn't made an effort to get out of Russia? In our town people live without windows, and the temperature dips below minus thirty. Factories have closed, and the only options are to drink yourself to death or migrate."

"Okay, okay."

"You always go on as if you've got all the answers," she says. "Try to imagine, for a moment, that you're wrong."

I don't want to fight. "All right, I'm not always right."

"Uhuh."

"No, I'm serious," I reply. "1.46 is out of the question, but I won't get anywhere if I don't make an effort."

So I start running forty-five minutes a day in my room. Whenever I struggle with motivation, Svetlana invites herself over, lies on the bed with a stopwatch and times me while I do intervals. Afterwards she works on her acting chops, or at least that's what she calls her exercises. Humming. Wagging her tongue. Scrunching up her face. Then we make out, her fleshy skin soft and unpredictable beneath my fingers.

After Svetlana leaves one evening, Mum tells me she's experiencing chest pains.

"Dr. Olsen says I'm stressed and need to slow down," she says. "But it isn't practical. I don't have vacation time for another six months."

"John, make your mother a cup of tea," Dad demands. "Then take out the garbage before you go to work."

It drives me batty. Clean the bathroom. Vacuum the living room. Cut the lawn. Make sure you get to work on time.

Why can't they leave me alone? I just want to be left in peace. So I take a page out of Kulvinder's book and clam up.

I make my own meals, eat in my room and wash my own plates. I do my own laundry, clean up my own messes and ignore them both as much as possible.

Kulvinder is also at his wits' end. He's tried holding his temper in check and working diligently at the restaurant to earn Mummy's forgiveness. But neither one of us is any closer to convincing our folks to let us run with the club again.

He's also finding Jugs a handful.

"Steph's just too high-maintenance," he complains. "The other day she cried about Finch for over two hours. That's what I came back to from work. Two hours of non-stop blubbering."

"Svetlana's trying to convince her to go to counselling."

"That's highly improbable," he replies.

"The word's 'unlikely.'"

"'Improbable' will do." He winds a new Swiss wristwatch. "The last shrink she saw said he had to feel her up in order for her therapy to work."

"Maaan."

I don't see her around much these days. She's been sneaking in the window and crashing at Kulvinder's place.

"It's all too tabloid-trash for me," he says.

"That's pretty snobbish."

"Don't be daft," he responds.

Kulvinder and I finally talk to Sam. The meet in Calgary is coming up, and we're missing crucial track workouts.

Sam proposes a meeting with the folks.

It's like a peace summit. Mrs. Sharma, Mum and Dad sit on one side of an oval table, while Kulvinder and I are on the other with Sam mediating from the head.

It's a mess from the get-go. The parents are united in their resolve to see us severely punished. We're suitably repentant but determined to keep running. Sam blathers on and reads quotes from sheets of paper.

The breakthrough comes at the eleventh hour.

"The boys understand that what they did was wrong," Sam says. "They know that it stands in vast contrast to what we're about at Achilles Track Club. I'm for teaching your boys to become men. But not just on the track, in every phase of their life. Yes, school remains a priority. So, too, does family. These are the values that we at Achilles ascribe to." He pulls sheafs of paper from his folder. They're contracts for all of us to sign. "Did you know that I've met some of the great runners of our time? Kip Keino, for instance. He runs an orphanage. That's what he does. Still giving back after all those years he gave to his country on the track. He's a great man. One whose character was moulded by the struggles he experienced on the track. This is the kind of man I want your boys to become. Fully rounded. Respectful. Hard-working. Committed.

"Yes, they've done wrong. But they feel remorse for this. Haven't all of us had our youthful indiscretions? Let he who is without sin cast the first stone. Give them another chance and they will not let you down." He points emphatically to the fine print of his contract. "I will personally see to it. I will be on your boys at every turn.

"I know what you're thinking. They will learn nothing without suitable punishment. All right, a one-month suspension in which there will be no contact with the club. It's all down there. It'll give them time to get their priorities in order. It will also give them an opportunity to see precisely what price must be paid for fouling up. One month, and when they return I will meet with them once a week. There we'll talk about their progress in all areas of their lives.

"Forgive me for sounding sentimental here, but I look at you all and am touched by what I see. My wife, Kioko, and I have been trying to have children for the past year. Family is very important to us. It's the bedrock. Without family one is alone, and nothing can be accomplished on one's own. So I commend you on the way you disciplined them when you discovered their drinking. But I ask that we move on from here, that we set standards that we'll hold them accountable for. That we use . . ."

I suspect it's the sheer exhaustion of listening to him go on. The Sharmas and Kipligats sign on the dotted line, and we're granted a reprieve.

6

November.

Relief from the turmoil brings Kulvinder and me together in a way we haven't been since the cross-country race in September. We do all our workouts together and take the rest of the month to clean up our act. We prick our fingers, mix our blood and take an oath to commit to our goals.

Working out is in. Alcohol is out. School is of utmost importance, with university applications a must. Jugs and Svetlana . . . well, that's tricky.

"It isn't as if I don't have a life of my own," Svetlana says. "The audition at the Arts Club is in two weeks."

Even so, she's brilliant about supporting me. She comes to workouts with her homework and yells encouragement when I begin to lag behind the others. She sits through my elaborate post-mortems of each practice and often claims she doesn't think Kulvinder is more talented than me.

"He just wants it more than you do," she says. "The guy vomits after every workout."

I listen to her. Her work ethic reminds me of Koech. She spends hours shouting monologues into the wind at Locarno Beach, her design being to drop deeper into character. To preserve her larynx, she drinks only cayenne and lemon water, and she doesn't watch films but dissects them scene by scene.

So I work harder and, with her badgering, finally experience the sheer agony of immense effort. Lungs burning. Legs shrieking for oxygen as I tumble towards the first meet, where I will be fitter than I've ever been.

My relationship with her is a puzzle, though. I know she cares for me, but she has an odd way of showing it. For instance, she won't invite me over to her house.

"My parents are old-fashioned," she says. "They think I should wait till I'm at least eighteen before I get involved with anyone."

"You're not playing me, are you?"

"Don't be ridiculous," she snaps. "My parents are a lot of things, but they're not racist."

The parental snub wouldn't burn me as much if she didn't act coy around taking the physical stuff to the next level. For instance, whenever I get up the courage to go anywhere beneath her navel, she slaps my hand away. "I said no flicking way."

"Come on, Svetlana," I urge. "I could die of blue balls."

"You need to finish reading . . ." It could be any one of those texts she says I could learn a thing or two from. Thick books written by raving separatists, who fill her mind with words and statistics I have no counter-arguments for.

That isn't all.

We have wicked fights. One time because I refuse to accompany her to see a ten-hour Fassbinder film. Another time because we argue over whether French food is more fattening than Italian.

However, it's the strangest thing. Although her quirks drive me crazy, I'm also intrigued by them. Like the time she introduced me to the paintings of Jean-Michel Basquiat. They had all these scribbled-out words and clumsy stick figures. Brilliant stuff. But we broke up temporarily when she showed up with the "Angry Penis Sketches." A collection of cocks that she crossed out or dismembered in some way.

As difficult as it is to admit, the toughest part of being with her doesn't have much to do with who she is. It's more about other people. She's pudgy, and I sometimes feel ashamed showing her any public affection.

Kind of shallow, but there it is.

I'm exhausted from a work shift and don't remember falling asleep.

At around three o'clock in the morning there's a loud knock on the window. It's Jugs, blasted out of her tree.

I take her by the forearms and lift her inside.

"Erica told Kulvinder to split on me," she mumbles. "She says my problems can't be his."

I yawn. "He told you that?"

"He didn't have to, a woman knows." She lies down on the bed. "Trust me. A woman knows."

"It's three o'clock, Steph. Can't we talk about this tomorrow?"

"Do ya know people at school call me a skank?" I sit beside her. "They think I led Finch on. Can you believe that?"

"Your friends believe you."

"Do you, Leeds?"

I haven't made up my mind yet. "Of course I do, silly."

She grins. "Know what they said about Stephanie? Remember, the one I talked about? I'm Steph. She's Stephanie." I nod. "They said she went down on the ice-hockey team. Ain't that whack? God, I miss her. We were like sisters."

She's talking too fast, and there's sweat on her upper lip.

"Guess what?" she asks.

"What?"

"Guess."

"How many of those blue pills did you take?"

"Those pricks at Social Services are sniffing around again."

I touch her forehead. "How many pills?" It's burning up.

"Two. Four." She shuts her eyes. "Lots of tequila."

"Goddamnit, Steph."

I lug her to the bathroom, fill the tub with cold water and lift her in, fully-clothed.

When I dunk her head in, she squeals.

There's knocking on the bathroom door. "What's going on in there?" Dad demands.

"Stephanie's not doing so well," I reply.

"Let me in," Mum says.

I dunk Jugs under again. "I got it, Mum." She emerges from the water sputtering. "She'll be okay."

There's silence on the other side of the door. "Have you two been drinking?" Dad asks.

I fling open the door. "Want to check my breath?" I yell.

Jugs giggles.

Mum barges past.

"I said I got it," I repeat.

Mum pries open Jugs' eyelids. "It looks like she'll be okay if we keep her awake."

The Kipligats take turns dunking Jugs in the tub. It's the first time in a while we've done anything as a family.

As the meet quickly approaches, Svetlana and I take it upon us to keep an eye on Jugs. Kulvinder's got Calgary on the mind, and her brush with an overdose decreases his interest in being around her.

"I don't need a pill-popping junkie in my life." We're at the restaurant; he washes plates while I dry. "She'll only take me down with her."

"But she's your girlfriend, man."

"When it comes to this drug business, the best thing to do is hide your valuables and make yourself scarce."

My face gets hot. "She's not a toy you throw away once you've grown tired of it."

"Listen, she's all yours," he replies.

I upend a bucket of plates onto the floor.

"Hey." It's Joginder, the head chef. "This is a workplace."

"You have no idea how easy you have it." I want to slug Kulvinder. The bloke takes everything for granted: his talent, his luck with women, the works. "You get what you want and think that makes you better than most people."

"What are you talking about?"

I hate working my ass off and never putting a dent in the distance between us. "Snob."

"Insufferable hypocrite," Kulvinder replies.

"You're just like your dad."

Kulvinder shrugs. "Look who's talking."

"Those broken dishes will be coming out of your paycheque," Joginder interrupts.

"I'm not cleaning that mess up," complains Ranjith, Joginder's protégé.

I throw my apron on the floor and head for the back door.

When I get home, Slim is waiting on the front steps. He's been developing a bizarre fixation on me of late. "Look it, Leeds. I can do a cartwheel with my mouth full." He crams his mouth with as much bread as possible before flipping through the yard.

"Good stuff." I'm weary. "You should join the circus."

"Wanna see it again?"

"Why not?" At least this time he didn't bring a squirrel he'd tortured to death with matchsticks.

When he's finished, I let him hang around, looking through running magazines, while I stew about how much I hate Kulvinder.

The Sharmas stop by for supper and it doesn't take long for the grown-ups to thrash around a load of batty comments.

"You lads are the future of this fine country." Mr. Sharma is stout, wears a white turban, a tweed jacket with patches on the elbows, and has a red ascot around his neck. "You'll be expected to adapt and to develop inviolable skills towards this end."

"These young people are so fortunate." Mrs. Sharma is wrapped from head to toe in layers of swirling cloth. "When I met Emmanuel, he didn't even know how to use a spanner."

"Must you always tell people this, Kuldip?" He's into the second bottle of wine he brought with him.

"It's nothing to be ashamed of," she continues. "These kinds of things were foreign to us. Nowadays toddlers who can program computers show up at Emmanuel's shop."

"Not quite toddlers." Mr. Sharma laughs.

"Close enough," she replies.

Mum and Dad dart in and out of the discussion. They're livelier than usual, and I enjoy watching them. At some point Dad and Mr. Sharma sing hymns from their boarding-school days, and Mum and Mrs. Sharma steal away for a quiet chat. When the women return, Mum makes an announcement.

"John, you can go to Treetops," she says.

Kulvinder and I smile at one another. It'll be great. I'll get to walk with gun-toting forest rangers and see elephants up real close.

"The hotel is in the Aberdare Forest, Son." Dad grins. "This means you'll get to see the bundu where the Mau Mau freedom fighters hid from the British during the struggle for Independence."

"Freedom fighters!" Mr. Sharma chortles. "That's some euphemism. Those people were thugs."

It looks, for a moment, like Dad's going to plunk him one. Veins pop up at his temples. "Thugs!"

Mr. Sharma swallows half a glass of wine. "When my father came to this country, Nairobi was a swamp with a railway station. There were no roads or even schools to speak of. But he saw possibilities, and he started a tailoring business." He refilled his glass. "He was industrious and in time established Sharma's Ltd., but all he ever heard from Natives was how Asians had a stranglehold over their trade opportunities." His hand shook, and wine spilled onto his fingers. "The Europeans were the ones who controlled the Legislative Council and claimed the White Highlands as Crown land. The Europeans implemented the burdensome Hut and Poll

Tax." He glanced at Kulvinder. "But you know what, in 1953, during the State of Emergency, Natives who'd taken the Mau Mau's oath set fire to our shop." Mrs. Sharma removes the glass from his trembling hand. "We lost everything. And why? Because that ilk you indecorously describe as Freedom Fighters claimed that Africa was for the Africans, even though we'd contributed mightily to build this land. Even though this is our country as well."

Everyone clams up.

"I'll get the pudding," I say.

"Good idea," Mum replies.

"No," Dad interjects. "I want the boy to hear this." He leans forward in his seat. "When I was a younger man, I worked as a clerk in a shop run by a certain Mr. Ravji.

"Whenever the Wazungu supervisor came by for an inspection, I suddenly couldn't do anything right by Ravji.

"'Kipligat, I wanted an order of thirty cans of beans, not twenty.' Or, 'I have no idea what they taught you at school. But it's well below the acceptable standard.'

"One day the supervisor noticed a discrepancy in the books. 150 shillings weren't accounted for. A meeting was called, and Ravji told him he'd seen me take money from the till.

"What nonsense. I'm no thief. I worked for everything I own.

"Two weeks later I was summoned to court in front of a Wazungu magistrate, and it was Ravji's word against mine.

"I spent the next twelve months in jail. Twelve months, and I'd done nothing wrong. So don't talk to me about how tough Asians had it. You didn't get fingerprinted and have to carry around a kipande card. You didn't get uprooted from your ancestral land. In fact, without African self-government we'd still be your lackeys."

The room aches with tension.

"Lots of Asians and Africans worked together during the struggle for independence," Mum says. "M.A. Desai, the editor of the East African Chronicle, helped Harry Thuku get reductions in the Hut and Poll Tax, remember?"

"I agree with Gladys," Mrs. Sharma adds. "It's a shame to see these matters discussed solely in adversarial ways. That's only part of the story. My sense is we ought to be grateful that after all that history, the four of us can sit here and share a drink."

"I propose a toast," Mum says.

The women lift their wine glasses and wait for the men to join them.

"You took my glass away, Kuldip," Mr. Sharma mumbles.

"Here," she replies.

"Mine's empty," Dad mutters.

Mum refills his glass for him.

"To friendship," Mum toasts.

Everyone except Dad and Mr. Sharma clink their glasses.

I think about Dad in handcuffs and look away from Kulvinder. We're so different. Not just in the way his family eats roast beef and Yorkshire pudding at the Norfolk Hotel every Sunday, or the way they own more houses than we do. It's more than that: it's talk that doesn't come out right, shabby feelings at the bottom of the gut, awkwardness that makes it impossible to look one another in the eye—Dad and Mr. Sharma, Kulvinder and I.

7

Two days before the meet starts, Kulvinder, Erica, Vivian and I arrive in Calgary. Sam couldn't get time away from work, but he's put Erica in charge.

"We're here to race," she says. "Try to keep that uppermost in your minds."

We fall in line. Banishing the notion of lollygagging beneath the lamplight along Electric Avenue. Opting instead to spend our time relaxing in the hotel.

Kulvinder and I are still on the outs and solve the sticky problem of rooming together by spending time apart. I watch the telly in the room while he disappears poolside with Erica.

On the second day the heats are a cinch for everyone but Erica. Her left hamstring has been tight, and she jogs off the track after 200 metres.

"I was afraid if I pressed, I'd pull," she says at dinner.

"What you did was sagacious," Kulvinder replies.

"Hey, forget about that. It's your birthday today."

I'd forgotten. "Happy Birthday," I mutter.

"You're getting to be an old man," Vivian says.

"We ought to go celebrate instead of sitting around in the hotel," Erica says.

"Are you fuckin nuts?" Vivian replies. She isn't about to violate her parole. "The finals are at nine tomorrow." Information we already know. "I'm turnin the fuck in at ten."

"Kulvinder, what do you say?" Erica's hand is resting on his thigh. "We'll go out for a couple of hours and be back by eleven."

"I'm a little susceptible right now," Kulvinder says. "We leave at six tomorrow, and I still haven't experienced any of Calgary's vaunted night life."

Sagacious! Vaunted Night Life! He has Erica-itis again. "I don't think it's such a good idea myself," I say. "We're here to race, remember?"

"Jesus!" Kulvinder exclaims.

"Don't 'Jesus' me," I reply.

"Time out." Erica bangs a fist on the table. "I'm tired of all this tension between you. We're supposed to be a team."

I stare at my plate of spaghetti.

"Getting out together will be a way to kiss and make up," Erica presses.

"It won't do to go messing with your routine so close to the finals," Vivian warns.

"Sod it," Kulvinder replies. "It's my birthday for crying out loud."

The three of us show up at the Rhizome early. The plan is to stay for a couple of hours then take a cab back to the hotel.

There's a short line-up in front of a bouncer decked out in a black tuxedo. His bloated shoulder muscles make it impossible to tell where his neck is.

"I may be a wee toight tonoight," the fellow in front of us says to his friend. "I didn'a cash me travellers' cheques."

The friend, a brother, pulls out a wallet. "Don't sweat it." Hands him a number of crisp bills. "Check out the doublicious in the tank top."

The Brit sneaks a look back at Erica, who's taken to staring at her reflection in a window.

The line shifts quickly, leaving the ogling pair standing in front of the bouncer.

"Breeeent!"

"Tiiiino!"

"Come in, come in." They vanish inside. "Next." We step towards him, and I root among crumpled bills for the phony driver's licence Vivian lent me.

The bouncer barely glances at it. "Okay."

I wait for the others at a counter where a woman wearing a fake leopard-skin coat collects cash.

"That'll be eight dollars." She's poker-faced. Focused on the task at hand. Red lipstick smeared on her front teeth as money changes hands.

Erica orders a rum-and-coke. Kulvinder, the jackass, follows suit.

Sam will kill us if he finds out. "Ummmm . . ." The bartender doesn't have all day. But I don't know what to do. This is a chance to clock a decent time, for Christ sake. Why mess that up? "Do you have . . . Scotch?" One drink won't do any harm.

"Sure. On the rocks?"

I'm slow to reply. "When was the last time you had a drink without ice?" Erica asks.

We all laugh.

It takes a few minutes before the bartender re-emerges with our orders.

"This round is on me." Erica says, paying up. She then bounces change into a small tip glass beside the cash register. "Happy Birthday, Kulvinder." She plants a kiss on his lips.

"To turning seventeen." I lift up my glass.

"Down the hatch," Erica adds, draining her glass. I take a sip—gag—and drink a little more.

A music video plays on screens scattered around the bar. Big Daddy Cane grinds before a backdrop where bikini-clad hoochies shake ass in a jeep. Quite uninteresting really, so I concentrate instead on the steady trek of over-the-hill thirtysomethings trickling into the club.

Mustached men whose hair is slicked back with gel gesture dramatically. They wear matching suits of cream and beige, gold watches, trunk jewellery and shiny black shoes. Others are dressed-down, as if in response. They natter in clumps packed into dimly lit corners of the bar.

"You're falling behind, Leeds," Kulvinder says, ordering us another round. His look says, loosen up will ya, it's my fucking birthday.

Erica's right. We're a team. It isn't helping to be at one another's throats on the road. Kulvinder and I can sort out our differences when we get back to Vancouver. In the meantime, all I have to do is keep track of the time.

I give him money and go back to work on my Scotch.

It goes down like foul-tasting mouthwash.

Brothers hipped to the limit roam the outer regions of the room. They stand near clusters of women who've prepared long and hard for the evening. Their hair is smeared with mousse.

"Down the hatch," Erica says, and we demolish the second round.

My fingers tingle pleasantly, and I'm light-headed, a sensation that leaves me slow to react when the fellas from the line-up lean against the bar beside us.

The brother leans forward to whisper into Erica's ear and flashes a fifty-dollar bill.

"No thanks." She slides her hand into Kulvinder's.

The brother shrugs, purchases two drinks equipped with umbrellas and moves on.

He doesn't have to go far. Two women sit farther down the bar. One has struggled into a skintight blue dress, and the other is wrapped in a thigh-hugging lime-green number.

"Can my friend and I buy you ladies a drink?" he asks.

They giggle before Blue responds from beneath her blonde bouffant. "Why the hell not?"

"What'll it be then, luv?"

She points to the wall where a list of shots hangs. "I'd like an Orgasm."

Lime-Green covers her face with her hands.

"Wouldn't you prefer a Long Screw?" the brother returns.

"No," Blue laughs. "We'd take an Orgasm over a Long Screw any day."

I break away for a piss; the drink's gone straight through me. I return to catch the tail end of what appears to have been a successful pull.

Kulvinder suggests that we hit the dance floor.

"That would be cool," Erica replies. "I can't feel a thing in my hamstring since I got those drinks into me."

"You coming, Leeds?"

"Nah, you two go ahead." I don't want to be a party to Kulvinder's betrayal of Jugs. "I'll be fine. There are worse things than sitting in a nightclub alone."

Kulvinder and Erica are the only ones on the dance floor. Her tank top exposes a belly button above hips that brush Kulvinder's faded jeans.

Man, I should leave. Instead I order one Scotch-on-the-rocks after another.

"Leeds."

"Yeh."

"I don't think you're a Native." *Kulvinder and I sit on the floor in my bedroom. It's the first time we've played since our dads' squabble. He stares at the wall on which I've taped an old clipping of Mike Boit, the 800-metre specialist, crossing the finish line as the first African to break the 3.50 barrier in the mile.* "You're different."

"I know."

We get silent.

"Want some spearmint gum?" *he asks.*

"Sure."

He hands me a stick.

"Koech gave me these." They're copies of Track and Field
News. *"Wanna read one?"*

"Okay."

We lie beside one another on our bellies, read and chew gum.

"Another drink?" It's a waitress with platinum-blonde hair.

"No thanks," I reply.

DJ Fab Live Freestyle is playing real danceable music.
Svetlana would love it here. The guy is serious. Switching his
attention from one turntable to another. Spinning from one
freshly minted jam to the next, a headphone propped on the
side of his head as he works out the scratch breaks.

By the time I work up the nerve to wade out to an empty
space on the dance floor, I'm hammered.

The music curls up behind me like a forty-foot wave. I wait
until it slips under me, tows me out into its wake. My arms
stretch out, my body cuts loose and I ride forward—buck wild—
out of sync. Fab Live Freestyle's shout-outs and sampled funk
deposit me into the belly of the groove.

The next sequence is hazy. One minute I'm humping the
backbeat. The next, fingers dig into my shoulder, and my eyes
open to the sight of the neckless bouncer, who drags my ass off
the dance floor.

"Hey."

His fingers dig deeper into my flesh.

"Hey."

Blue and the brother scatter out of harm's way.

"What the fuck?"

"Faggot," he hisses.

I shove hard and knock him into Lime-Green—an accident—and they tumble to the floor, a pair of dolls.

"What the hell are you doing?" It's the Brit, who's lost his accent. "That's my lady you're fucking with, arsehole."

"This is a party, people." The brother tries to calm everyone down. "A party."

The bouncer leaps up, enraged. We circle one another, and I search, over his massive body, for an exit to tumble through.

"Come on, cocksucker," he says.

I don't have time to think. I just put my fists up in the air and prepare for the pummelling to begin.

"Please, sir." A man in a suit pushes his way between us. "I'm the manager. A word with you." I drop my fists, gather myself and follow him. "I'm sorry. I don't allow people to dance alone." He's agitated. "There are so many pretty girls. I'm sorry. We don't allow people to dance alone." A trace of an accent indicates a connection to Italy. "It's club policy. You must understand."

"What planet are you from?" Kulvinder joins the fray now that Erica has seen how he can handle a crisis with such sexy cool.

"Please. If he must dance alone, I'm going to have to ask him to leave." The manager is flanked by two other neckless chumps.

"Erica Holt," she extends a hand. "I'm an officer with the Alberta Human Rights Commission. Your policy is a violation of the Code."

"No. Please. I must ask him to leave." The manager plays with a thick gold ring that hangs from a gold chain at his neck.

"Fine then," I shout. "I'll see your cracker-ass in court."

"Suit yourself. I run a classy operation. There are beautiful girls here."

I hurry past them, indignant now that my prettier-than-average-face won't get stomped through the floor.

It's a relief to emerge beside a line-up of the well-groomed chattering outside.

"Is it crowded?" someone asks.

"Boycott the damn place," Erica replies.

We're silent as we clump, soused, back to the hotel.

Fuck, it's 1:30. There are eight and a half hours until the race.

8

I don't know how I make it through the warm-up. But I wind up puking under the stands ten minutes before the race.

"Are you okay?" It's Vivian, on her way to the warm-up area for the women's 400.

"Yeah." I wipe my mouth in embarrassment.

"Are you sure?"

"Yeah. Thanks."

"I have to go check in."

"I know. Break a leg."

"You too."

I go back to my dry heaves before heading out to find Kulvinder stalking the warm-up area and looking composed. A surprise, considering he crawled back into the room at five o'clock.

We do a series of easy accelerations on the infield of the 200-metre track while the race gets underway.

Vivian gets a good start and appears to be running a smart race until she stumbles coming off the second bend. She somehow manages to stay on her feet.

"Don't panic," Kulvinder mutters when Vivian begins to press. Not a bad move, it turns out, since she comes off the final bend in first place.

Her arms and shoulders tighten.

"Relax," Erica yells from the bleachers. "Relax."

Vivian's face loosens, and she strides up the straight with half a step on her closest competitor.

The rest will just have to be guts and technique until she crosses the finish line.

The unofficial clock beside the track has her at 54.78. It's a whopping personal best.

It isn't long before the starter calls us together for our race. I take off my lucky sweat top while he reads names from a list of competitors.

I've drawn lane eight. A drag because I won't be able to see the field behind me.

I don't remember much about what happens next, although I do recall struggling around the first bend.

The first 200 is an insane twenty-three seconds, and I just can't keep up. Not the way I feel, anyway. I'm running in quicksand, watching the others pull away.

My body refuses to give chase, and I become a spectator to the race.

Kulvinder, no doubt juiced by his late night bonk with Erica, tries to put the thing away early. His big move coming with 500 to go.

Three runners go with him. Some skinny fellow from Manitoba, a farmer's kid from Saskatoon, a 400-metre specialist from Quebec and Philip Lawlor, the favourite, who is running confidently in front of his home crowd.

They split the quarter in fifty-three point something, and I'm three seconds behind.

Kulvinder throws in a second spurt with 300 to go, and by the time they're into the bell lap, they've dropped the fellow from Quebec.

It suddenly occurs to me, as I watch this taking place, that I'm gaining on them.

I can hear Sam's voice repeating, "Stay focused on your form. Not the way you're feeling, but your technique."

The gap is down to two metres with one hundred left. I think of Koech. He'd tell me I can get through this.

"Stay tall, Leeds," I hear Vivian yell. "Stay tall!"

I begin to lift my knees and pass the spent 400-metre specialist as we head into the homestretch. My next target is the tight pack of three runners who are staggering towards the finish. I feel the way Koech looked the day he WHOOOSHED. WHOOSH: I run wide and am shoulder to shoulder with the lot, thirty to go. That's when my legs begin to feel like jelly.

It takes a photo to unscramble the order at the finish.

I phone home as soon as we make it back to the hotel.

Hey, Dad. What's up? The weather here has been nothing short of brilliant. Lots of snow but still sunny. Light breeze. No complaints. What? Oh, the race. Not bad. Yeah, it went well. Please. No need to apologize. Dad! Come on. It's water under the bridge. Let's just be glad we've got each other, shall we?

He answers on the first ring, "Hello."

"Hey, Dad."

"Where have you been, Son? We hoped to hear from you last night."

"Dad . . ."

"Listen, I've got some bad news. Your mum was admitted to the hospital last night."

"Oh, God."

"She's having chest pains and hasn't been able to keep her food down. Thank goodness they didn't find a problem with her x-rays. But blood tests show her enzyme count is high, and she'll have to stay in Intensive Care until she stabilizes . . ."

Koech staggers into the living room.

I figure he's drunk. That is, until Mum rushes over to help him to the sofa. "What in God's name, Koech?"

Dad hovers over them. "John," he barks. "Get the First Aid kit from the bathroom."

By the time I return, Koech is stripped down to his undies. Blood has dried in clumps around his swollen right knee.

Mum wraps it in a wet flannel.

"John," she says. "There's a bandage beneath the sink."

Koech is crying, and Mum rubs the swelling with an ice cube. Dad paces in front of them and wrings his hands.

"We were peacefully demonstrating against bulldozing the slum," Koech sobs. "But the police began clubbing everyone in sight, then they threw canisters of tear gas."

Mum pulls a batch of cotton from the First Aid kit and dabs it with peroxide. "This will sting a little." She gently wipes the antiseptic into a long gash. "Ahab!" Mum wraps a bandage around Koech's leg. "We'll have to take the boy to the hospital. He'll need stitches."

"Did you put him up to this?" Dad demands.

"I'm as surprised as you are," Mum replies.

"Bloody hell, the deal with the Weaver Consortium is done."

"Ahab! This isn't the time."

"Right, the hospital," he mumbles. "I got it."

Later that night there's a soft knock on my bedroom door.

It's Dad. "Koech is going to be okay. He just has to stay at the hospital a couple of nights."

"How's his knee?"

"He'll live, but it doesn't look as if he'll run again this season." Dad's eyes are cloudy and dull. "Now get some sleep." He hugs me, his heart thumping against mine.

"Son! Son! Are you there?"

"Uhuh."

"You'd think with the money these bastard doctors make, they'd take more than ten seconds to answer a bloody question," Dad says.

"I'll be home by nine."

"We'll be at St. Paul's."

9

Mum gets fed liquids through an IV jabbed in the back of her hand while another tube, which supplies her with oxygen, is stuck in her nose. She's medicated, and her eyes are glazed.

"Hello, John," she says.

I sit down on her bed. "Hey, Mum. It looks as if you've been having a rough go of it."

A patient moans behind a curtain in another part of the unit.

"She's had a difficult day," Dad says. "But they gave her something to help her sleep." His eyes are red and his eyelids puffy. "Let's just hope she doesn't end up hooked on Valium like that Elizabeth Taylor woman."

"Don't be silly." It takes an effort for Mum to speak. "You're all making far too much of this." She's gaunt and kicks at her sheets. "How did your race go, Son?"

"Fine. Kulvinder won in 1.59.98, and I was tied for second with some guy from Ottawa. We both ran 2.00.02."

Her mouth opens as if she's about to say something. Then it closes. She grimaces and leans over the side of the bed. Dad grabs a pan, which he puts up to her face. He holds her head while she vomits.

Eventually she lies back on the pillow while Dad cleans spittle from the sides of her mouth with a cloth.

"Should I call a nurse?" I ask.

"No." Mum closes her eyes.

The only light in the room comes from the nurse's station in a hallway beyond the curtain. I can hear two of them talking about the number of guests that will be attending an upcoming wedding.

The tube in Mum's nose hisses; her eyelids begin to flutter, and a green pebble drops from her hand to the floor.

"Sweetheart," Dad squeezes her fingers. Her eyeballs roll upward. "Gladys." There's no response; tiny slits reveal the whites of her eyes. "Gladys!" He squeezes harder this time.

The corners of her mouth twitch, her eyes open and her eyeballs roll back into place.

"I'm so tired," she sighs.

Dad begins to cry and I sit on her bed. I hold the pebble and pull on the drawstring of Koech's hood.

In the morning I hear Dad bark into the phone. "What do you mean, they checked him out of the hospital? No. No. I didn't give my permission. No. I don't know anyone by that name."

In my pyjamas, I hurry to the sitting room to find Mum tugging on his arm.

"What's going on?" she asks.

"Nobody knows where Koech is," he replies.

I spend the rest of the day wrapped in a blanket on the sofa. I have a dull ache in my head and no appetite for food. The whole day, Mum and Dad have been out trying to track down Koech.

When they return in the evening they are both red-eyed.

Mum pulls me down beside her. "We've got some bad news, dear." She squeezes my shoulder hard and it hurts. "Men claiming to be police officers took Koech from his hospital room during the night."

"We've checked every station," Dad says. "But he's nowhere to be found."

My legs start to tremble, and I can't swallow.

"I'm going to keep calling around until I get some answers," Dad continues. "The boy can't have disappeared into thin air."

Muscles twitch around my mouth.

The crackpot squad of rotating medical staff isn't able to pin down the problem. "It's probably caused by an infection," Dr. Collins says before indulging in a bunch of medical goboldygook. "Her CKMB and MB indexes aren't elevated, which is a good sign. But her hemoglobin count is on the low side. Approximately 4.5. This shouldn't be any cause for concern. We find this generally to be the case with women. We'll continue with the antibiotics to bring her enzyme count down and clear any possible infection."

In the morning Kulvinder, Mrs. Sharma and Svetlana join us at her bedside.

Mum's face is ashen in the sunlight, and white grunge encircles her lips.

"Water," she croaks.

Dad is quick to hold a cup and straw to her mouth.

I touch her fingers, stare at a spot of blood on the bandage holding the IV in place.

"Man," Kulvinder says. "I forgot the, uh, card in the car."

"It's sticking out of your jacket pocket," Svetlana replies.

Mum starts coughing yellow vomit, and Mrs. Sharma holds the pan up for her. "It'll be okay, Gladys," she says.

When Mum lies back on the pillow, blood bubbles from her lips.

"Nurse," Dad shouts.

The rest of us scatter into the hallway. "Nurse," we scream. "Nurse."

A nurse hurries into the room and checks her pulse.

"Out," she demands. "Get out."

We file out of the room.

"Dr. Collins to I.C.U.," a voice blasts over the intercom. "Dr. Collins to I.C.U."

The four of us sit in the lobby. Svetlana has her arm around my shoulders; Kulvinder fidgets beside me, and Mrs. Sharma holds Dad's hand.

After forever, Dr. Collins emerges with a clipboard. "She's stable. She had a reaction to the penicillin . . ." I don't hear any more. Svetlana's fingers make the back of my neck tingle.

Mum's improvement is gradual but steady.

She's cheerful, even though she ends up in a room with a crabby stroke victim and her meals consist of vanilla-flavoured drinks.

Svetlana turns out to be real cool. Making time to be there when I need someone to unload on, stopping by the hospital to entertain Mum.

One thing starts to bug me, though: Jugs doesn't make an appearance. After all, Mum's bailed her out of several jams. It's the least she can do.

On Sunday, six days after Mum's admission, I hear Svetlana laughing in the hospital room.

I sidle up to the door.

"I found John hiding under the bed," Mum says. "He'd painted his body with white house paint."

Svetlana cracks up again.

"When I dragged him out, you know what he said?"

"What?"

"Look, Mum. I'm a *Wazungu*."

I hurry into the room.

"Mum!"

Svetlana can't stop laughing.

"Don't tell her anything; she's doing research for a part," I continue.

"What part?" Mum asks.

"Tell her," I say.

Svetlana blushes. "It's this story about a Ukrainian teenager who's been adopted by a Canadian family."

"It's a principal role at the Arts Club," I interrupt.

"Let the girl finish," Mum says.

"The director's set the play in the late nineteenth century, and he's experimenting with multicultural casting. The mother's being played by a First Nations woman . . ."

Don't get me wrong. I'm absolutely thrilled for Svetlana. Her hard work is paying off. However, I worry about Mum and her getting too chummy. I'm still ambivalent about her. There are other women in the world. Models. Dancers. Other athletes. But if Mum and her are close, they'll pressure me into getting hitched.

After leaving the hospital Svetlana and I go to Starbucks. She orders a latte with steamed milk, and I have a large black coffee.

"There's a table back there." I point to one beside the can.

"I'd rather wait for a window seat to open up," she replies.

We stand around sipping our drinks.

"Why didn't you ever tell me your dad used to be in politics?" she asks.

I shrug. "There isn't much to tell."

"That's hard for me to believe."

I change the subject. "Did you know, I never take cream in my coffee? Strong and black all the way for me."

"Heck, Leeds."

"I won't drink white wine either. Only red. Not white. Red."

She licks foam from her upper lip. "What's with you today?"

She needs to back off. I don't like feeling obligated to disclose everything about myself to her. Anyway, she's forgotten our first conversation, when she ran a guilt trip on me about our European car. "Nothing."

"Listen, there are things I'm not proud of."

"Yeh?"

"Yeah, like changing my name."

My mouth drops open.

"Don't look so shocked," she says. "Lots of actors do it. If I want to read for a variety of parts, I can't send out resumes as Svetlana Petrovskaya. I'll get called for auditions only when a production is looking for a Slav."

I point. "A table." I rush past a slow-moving thirtysomething couple and plop down by the window.

"Well?" I ask. "What's it going to be?"

She runs a finger over the cup's rim, and her features tighten. "Veta Peters."

"Veta Peters!"

"I know it still needs work."

I crack up.

"Don't be an asshole."

"Sorry."

"You have no idea what goes on in this business. God, how often do you see an actress with my build make a career out of this? Not often, right?" Man, she's usually so sure of herself. "I have to make compromises."

"I just think you're getting ahead of yourself," I say. "I mean, you're going to study at the National Theatre in Moscow someday."

She chews on her lip. "I'm running out of time."

"Come on, Svetlana. You're sixteen."

"Well, Papa wants me enrolled in the Engineering Department at U.B.C. next fall."

Shit, the floodgates are open.

Svetlana unplugged is more than I can handle right now. All I really want is to relax, wearing a cable-knit sweater and learning to play Pontoon. Instead I sit across from her as she unravels into secrets about run-ins with Papa.

After a fortnight Mum returns from the hospital. She's lost close to thirty pounds.

The entire experience spooks Dad. He morphs into a creature I hadn't known before. Forgetful. Unable to remember why he enters a room. A wildness creeps in at the edge of his eyes.

He begins watching everything they eat. Keeping it simple. Plying her with plenty of water, lots of fruit, grains and vegetables, and brisk walks afterwards.

He even gets himself a job as a janitor at a local high school.

It's time for the Kipligat men to step it up a notch.

DECEMBER:
Stepping It Up

1

High school is enough of a struggle without all the stress of late. I need to get my grades up from D's to B's. Low marks won't do me any good, even if scouts decide their lives have no purpose without me.

Kulvinder's already begun talking of a major, mathematics, with a minor in philosophy.

"I'm really getting into applying mathematical principles to some reading Erica's got me doing on logical positivism," he said. "The values we live by are human constructions. Meaning is dependent on whether these values can be logically validated."

"Life is one big calculus problem to you," I replied.

"Uhuh."

Since Calgary the guy's taken an extra fancy to his own self. But who can blame him? He's broken two minutes, and it's still early in the season.

When I complain to Svetlana, she accuses me of being puerile—something I get hot about after I look the word up in the dictionary.

I track Kulvinder down at recess. "Listen," I say. "Want to check out a movie at the Film Fest later tonight? Svetlana's got a rehearsal, and I don't particularly want to go home after practice."

"Sorry, mate." Mr. I'm-so-fucking-flash leafs through his latest purchase, a day-timer. "Can't make it out until next Thursday. Erica and I are going to Giceppe's for dinner tonight. There's that essay on *Portrait of the Artist as a Young Man* I have to get cracking on by Tuesday. Wednesday we're going to find a duvet cover for her futon. So Thursday after practice is the best I can do."

Erica's been pulling his strings about priorities. Heavy topics unrelated to either track or their burgeoning relationship don't hold his attention long.

"Oh. That may be a problem," I lie. "I've got research to do on that paper as well. Man, it's quite sad, but time just seems so limited these days."

"If you can't do it Thursday, there's the following Monday."

I cave. "No, Thursday is cool."

On Wednesday evening I toss my bags onto the mat at the front door after a half-decent workout of six eight-minute intervals over hilly terrain.

I'm running better workouts since Calgary. I've been consistent, and notice a definite improvement in my stamina. There haven't been any embarrassing ass kickings. No pitiful sightings of my sorry self bringing up the rear, planning a dramatic face-plant due to a tricky slipped disc. It's quite the opposite. Sam has even taken to saying how much of a goddamned stud I am, or words to that effect.

"Congratulations," he says, manhandling his second muffin while driving me to a bus stop. "Consider yourself a full-fledged member of Achilles Track Club."

I beam.

"Now there's no point in risking any more unnecessary injuries. We'll skip the rest of the indoor season and focus instead on building up to peak for Juniors in July." He wipes crumbs from his mouth. "Three spots on a team to Japan are there for the taking. I want you to think about whether any of them belong to you." He flips the tab off a soda and slurps it down. "Calvin Coolidge once said, 'Nothing in the world can take the place of persistence. Talent will not; nothing is more common than unsuccessful men with talent. Persistence and determination alone are omnipotent.'"

He reaches into a bag for another muffin.

"Understand?" he asks.

I nod.

"Open up the glove compartment," he says. "I have a surprise for you."

I turn the lock and pull out an envelope full of photographs.

"Keep the one on the top," he says.

It's a shot of the finish in Calgary. I'm in fourth place, straining towards the line, and Kulvinder is two feet ahead of me with his arms raised in triumph.

Sam reels into a verse from his track bible. "Remember, to be better Lots, you have to be Lots better."

I hate the quote and the photograph.

"Are you nervous about your two?" Koech asks.

"A little."

"That's natural." He insisted I take Kulvinder on, even if he does talk like Prince Charles. "Just remember to keep at it for 205 metres. It's important to run through the finish."

"Right."

"Don't give a damn about anyone else in the field."

"Don't give a damn."

He winks. "Now get out of the sun and rest your legs."

I lie in the shade under an oak tree, where I avoid the bees that rummage through the grass around me. I don't care where I finish, as long as Kulvinder doesn't beat me. That's what I'm nervous about.

At race time, I take my spot in lane four. Kulvinder's in lane three, and I can't see him. But Koech says I can use this to my advantage if I get out quick.

"It'll put pressure on him to chase you and force him to run your race instead of his."

The heat is suffocating.

"On your marks." I crouch on the ground. "Get set." I raise my backside. "Go." I sprint towards a distant ribbon.

The chalk sprinkled to mark each lane rises in clouds beneath the feet of the runner ahead of me. I accelerate until the muscles in my legs feel as if they'll rip, then I hold on. I'm a kite pulled into the blue sky. Wind carries me and I blast by the four athletes in the lanes outside of mine.

At about eighty metres my legs wobble on uneven ground. I decelerate, stumble over bumps and drift in towards lane three. When I try to pick up the pace again, my thighs get rubbery, and it's difficult to stay upright.

I hear Kulvinder creep up beside me.

Don't give a damn.

He moves level with me, thirty to go.

I close my eyes, put in one last burst and keep my legs moving. There's a loud cheer from the crowd, then I feel a ribbon across my chest. When I open my eyes, Kulvinder is a step behind me.

I shriek and raise my arms in the air.

Koech picks me up and whirls me around in the air. His smile reveals his teeth, all the way back to his molars.

"Now if only I could get you to train," he beams.

Complete strangers come over to tell me what a great race I ran, that I have a promising future ahead of me. After a while I can't take the attention anymore and hide behind the Assembly Hall.

When I walk around the corner of the building I bump into Kulvinder.

"Sorry," I backpedal.

He's scratching the blade of his Swiss Army knife into the wall.

"Good fucking race." He holds out a hand.

"Thanks." I check to see if there's snot smeared onto his palm. "Same to you."

"I thought I had the bugger by the balls."

"Me too," I reply.

I wander into the kitchen to find Mum and Dad unusually up-beat.

They go on about the smashing weather, warm fronts coming in from the West Indies, and make giggly contrasts between the temperatures in Mexico and that of say, Winnipeg.

I assume the worst.

After a blow-by-blow account of a drab tête-à-tête on CBC Radio that morning, they cut to the chase.

"Son, we went to see Dr. Olsen for a follow-up session, and he didn't have good news," Dad says.

"He says I have arteriosclerosis."

I fiddle with the drawstring on Koech's hood.

They could be saying anything—the bathroom needs a good scrub, or Mrs. Sharma is coming over for dinner. My eyes fasten on a dripping tap.

"There's nothing that can be done about it," Dad says. "We just have to hope for the best."

"I'm going to have to take time off work. No question about it. So it would be a great help if you found a job that pays better. I've talked to Kulvinder's mother, and she says all you need is to give her a week's notice."

I sit down and try to absorb what they just said.

"Sure." I'm suddenly dog-tired and talking gibberish. "No worries, Mum. You'll have Dad and I to spoil you to death. Sorry. I meant, to spoil you. That's what I meant. We'll spoil you silly. No worries."

I don't tell Svetlana about Mum. I've already loaded enough burdens on her. Anyway, I never quite know the point of revealing a hardship only to have the other person relate how they've been through some sort of equivalent experience. I don't want to be told of an aunt with a brain tumour, or a crack-addicted relative who jumped in front of a subway car. Nor do I want to be held tight or have the back of my neck stroked. I just want everyone to shut up, be quiet and leave me alone.

Mrs. Sharma mentioned it to Kulvinder, but I made him promise to keep it quiet. I'm too uncomfortable admitting to any sort of shabbiness around the team. After all, who wants to be the one constantly dragging the others down?

So I say nothing at the next practice. I just keep it inside, put it in a box somewhere in my chest and weld that puppy shut. There are other things that need my attention. For instance, the hill-work Sam has begun to integrate into our training regimen.

"All right, folks. It's crunch time," Sam announces. We limber up at the bottom of a 200-metre incline. "How's the knee, Vivian?"

"It'll be cool."

"Try the first one. See how it feels. Then we'll make a decision about whether or not you should continue." He consults with papers on a clipboard. "We'll be doing twenty reps with a 200 jog recovery between each and a six-minute break between sets."

"How fast?" Erica asks.

"About eighty-five percent. We shouldn't find ourselves unable to complete the last set."

We stretch a little more while he walks to the top of the hill, takes out his stopwatch and waits for us to begin.

The first three are a breeze. Even though Kulvinder, the cocky bastard, keeps kicking it up a gear over the final fifty.

He's really getting on my last nerve.

"Slow it down, guys," Sam says. "These aren't supposed to be at maximum effort."

Motherfuck that. If Kulvinder wants to race, I'll dust his ass.

We're both on the fly from the get-go on the next one, and at about fifty I press hard on the accelerator.

It hurts like a cocksucker, but he stays with me.

I push again at the half-way mark, and he counters by ratcheting it up a notch.

It's Sports Day all over again.

I can hear his garbled breath at my shoulder. If I can just throw one more surge at him, I'll break the arrogant tosser.

I pull ahead slightly when we hit the 180 mark, and I wind up finishing a foot ahead of him.

"That was 33.5 seconds, Leeds. At the rate you're both running, you won't have anything left for the second set."

I gather myself on the jog downhill. My quadriceps burn and I gulp for air. But I'm not about to pull back. No fucking way. I'm like a jumpy cheetah jacked up on the scent of impala meat.

We turn at the bottom of the hill. I raise my arm. "Ready." I drop it as we take off.

I make it about twenty metres, tip over on my right foot, tumble sideways onto the tarmac and scrape tracts of skin from the palms of my hands. "Shit." I roll onto my right side and grab my ankle.

It feels like I just shoved it through a plate of glass.

"You need to get that checked out." Sam watches it swell up and prods it with his fingers. "I'll have to take you to the Emergency before it gets any worse."

"I can flag down a cab," Vivian says. "My knee's toast, so it ain't no sweat for me to take him to the hospital."

"That's good of you, Vivian. That way we can still do a second set."

"Are you gonna be all right, Leeds?" Kulvinder asks.

"Yeah, it's probably just a sprain."

"Be sure to call me when you know what's up," Sam says.

"Sure, Coach."

"It probably makes sense to skip the Film Fest tonight," Kulvinder says.

"No. Go," I reply half-heartedly.

"All right," Erica says. "But call us later. Kulvinder will be over at my place."

No shit.

I have a partial tear in my Achilles tendon, an injury that will set me back at least six weeks. So I have to use a crutch, and Sam confines me to knocking off a bunch of boring drills in the swimming pool.

The following day Svetlana treats me to a steak dinner, then takes me for a ride in a cab. We drive through a light drizzle.

A shaggy, bearded brother steers with one hand on the wheel, his eyes searching the sidewalk for the latest in leggy action while he gabs away on a cell phone.

"When I went over on it, I heard a pop," I say to Svetlana.

"How much weight can you put on it?"

"None."

"Not to flip you out or anything, but . . ."

"You're going to anyway."

"One time a doctor told me I'd sprained my big toe. But it hurt like hell and kept swelling up. Finally I got it checked again. Guess what? Those flicking idiots hadn't seen I'd broken a bone."

"Your point being what?"

"No point," she says. "Just making conversation."

At length we arrive at an inn in the West End.

"Surprise," she announces. "I figured you needed to get away for a bit."

My jaw drops.

"Don't worry," she says. "Your parents think we're on an overnight field trip with our Canadian History class."

I wait in the room while she runs through the parking lot to a liquor store. Rain splatters in half-inch circles against the window.

Five minutes later she bobs into view. She tumbles into the room, rips off her wet jacket and burrows her head under my arm.

"Look," she says. "Red wine."

My socks stick to the inside of my shoes.

We wrap ourselves in a blanket and sit outside on the dry end of the balcony. Drinking. Staring at the torso-shaped grain in the banister's wood.

"My mum has arteriosclerosis," I say.

Beetles bump into the lamplight then fall among the elongated shadows that lie over the cracks on the lot's sloping tarmac.

"She told me already," Svetlana replies. "She felt you might need someone to talk to."

"I should've mentioned it earlier."

She kisses my hands, her mouth red and rusty and sullen, like dry pine leaves.

Soon I'm nattering away about my brother. "I had this eerie experience in Calgary," I confess. "There was this point on the home stretch where I was gaining on the field and, for an instant, it felt like I was Koech. Does that sound weird?"

"You can run faster than he did, you know."

I shake my head. "We've been through this. 1.46 is out of my league."

I notice her pupils, wet black orbs surrounded by a tiny ring of brown.

She slips out of the blanket and pulls me to the bed.

"It isn't," she insists.

Her forehead is sluiced with bangs, and her nipples poke up under her blouse.

She slides the soles of her feet over mine, and my eyes fixate on her body.

Suddenly our lips work fast against each other, her eyes hidden behind her dark hair, wine tingling on my tongue.

Our knuckles clack against the brass buckles of our belts.

"It isn't," she repeats.

I grab for her waist, tug off her jeans, wrench aside her panties and knead the mound above her pubic bone.

She moves against my fingers.

Her nails dig into the scars on my arms. One of her knees draws up and into my chest. My fist clutches her hair as our muscles contract, and I pull the back of her head into a swathe of moonlight.

I shudder, and her legs wrap around my waist.

Later the next day, I decide to surprise Svetlana with a slice of chocolate-swirl cheesecake. I've thought it through. Her dad may not want her to have a boyfriend, but he'll be certain to fall prey to my charm.

She lives in Mount Pleasant, in a neighbourhood of trailer-park-shaped houses. Country music plays in a couple of the homes, but the sidewalks are deserted.

I hobble up a pathway and knock on the door.

There's no answer, so I try again.

Floorboards creak. A bolt clicks. Then the door squeaks open a sliver, and a woman peeks out. "Ya."

I smile and show her the cake. "I'm here to see Svetlana. Is she home?"

"Svetlana," she yells.

Feet scamper down stairs.

Then the door bursts open and a round little man brandishes a baseball bat.

He lunges forward.

I fall backwards, dropping the cake. *Crack*. The bat hits the cement beside my head.

"Papa!" Svetlana climbs onto his back. "Stop." Her face is crimson. "That's my friend."

He shoves her inside then slams the door behind him.

"A black," he yells. "A flicking black."

I sit on the grass next to the upturned cheesecake until the racket in the house subsides.

When I get home, I lock myself in the bathroom, run a blade across my forearm and sit on the cold linoleum tiles as I watch it bleed.

In the living room a record needle skips, and my insides bang like an oil drum.

At supper time the family sits around the dinner table. Mum picks at her plate with a fork while Dad watches her, and I listen to the sound of myself eating.

It's a relief to be interrupted by the telephone.

"I got it." I limp to the kitchen.

"Kipligats' residence."

"Are you okay?" It's Svetlana.

"You lied."

"Why the hell did you come over?"

"You lied," I reply.

"I never give you grief about matters you don't want to discuss." Her old man starts to shout. "Damn, I got to go."

"Right."

"I love you, Leeds."

I swallow spit.

I seek out Jugs, knock on her door and find her flaked out in front of her TV.

"Anything interesting on?" I ask.

"*Seinfeld* rerun," she says. "Sit." She clears away an open box filled with pizza crusts.

"How's things?"

"The same ol' fucked," she replies.

I pick up an unauthorized biography of Elvis from the floor. "Elvis?"

"Ma's," she says. "Ever heard that song, *Love Me Tender*? Elvis sang it to Priscilla the first time they met. She was fourteen, and he was twenty-four. Wanna hear the first verse?"

"Not really."

"Love me tender, love me sweet . . ." She starts to cry.

"What is it, Steph, Kulvinder again?"

"Nah," she replies. "It's Ma. She jammed out on counselling, and now Slim's and me's s'pos'd to go to foster care next month."

"Gawd."

She launches into a long tirade: phobias and anxieties, random trains of thought loosely associated with one another.

By the time I wobble out of there, I realize she hasn't bothered to ask me how I've been doing. Again.

At school the next morning Svetlana suggests we skip our first class and talk.

We disappear into the woods behind the cafeteria.

"Why didn't you tell me about your dad?" I ask.

She unzips her fly and tugs down her jeans. There are bruises the size of potatoes on her thighs.

"Good Christ, Svetlana."

"That's his way of saying we can't see each other anymore."

I try to hug her, but she pushes me away.

"We're not going to be able to see each other anymore," she says.

"Fuck him."

"We don't have a choice."

"Listen, baby. I know it'll be rough, but we should go to the cops. The bastard ought to be charged with assault."

She shrinks away. "No flicking way," she objects. "It doesn't matter what we want. He doesn't want us to see each other anymore."

My stomach rumbles; my mouth is dry, and my fingers tremble. Continuing the conversation is too difficult. I can't muster up the energy to explain my way through any of it. What did I expect? If she wants to split, then split. Don't fucking waste my time with bullshit about Papa. "Fine," I say.

"It's not . . . what I mean is . . . I don't know how to say what I mean."

"Listen, like you said to Papa, I'm just your friend."

She flinches like I popped her one in the solar plexus, does up her fly and rushes off in the direction of school.

I count to ten. If she comes back I meant something to her.

"One, two, three, four, five, six, seven, eight, nine, ten."

3

Vivian's my saving grace.

Her knee gets worse, and Sam sends her off to join me in the pool. This is the only time I recall enjoying myself since splitting with Svetlana.

"We was so whacked on smack we didn't give two shits," Vivian says while we soak in the whirlpool after pushing through a series of knee lifts in the deep end. "As long as we got paid enough to cop, that was all that mattered."

"Wow."

I feel like such a cornball around her. Man, if I was her, I wouldn't talk to me.

"Snortin and shit was cool and all. But that ride got stale real quick. Jonesin till the next hit ain't no way to live."

She lifts herself out of the swirling water, sits on the edge and places the back of her knee in the path of a gushing jet stream.

"You've got such great attitude," I say. Bullshit flings out my mouth like rice on a bride. I'm so in awe that I make things up as I go along. "You never complain, and focus instead on what's possible."

She turns to allow the jet stream to massage the front of her kneecap.

"My man, Will, was in lockdown for a stretch. Him and a couple of shorties got snatched up for jacking rides. But that's ancient motherfuckin history now. We didn't wanna go out like that."

She climbs out of the whirlpool and waits poolside for me to join her in a session of abdominal strengthening crunches.

Vivian isn't like anyone I've ever known. She takes lithium for chronic depression, has a rap sheet as long as my arm and is a recovering alcoholic. Plus, she has a track record that makes me plenty insecure.

I'm just an ordinary sod. Sure I get pissed at the folks now and again, but otherwise my life is pretty lame.

I join her poolside and think about whether tattoos would make me seem more hard core.

Mum slips into a deep funk. She stays in bed most of the day, no longer does her daily prayers at her altar and only seems to get up when Mrs. Sharma stops by for a visit.

"Kulvinder's dating some girl I've yet to meet," Mrs. Sharma says over tea. "They spend all their time together, and I barely ever see him. I've warned him. I said, 'you must be careful about the girls here.' But you think he listens? The boy's going to wake up one day and find she's having his baby. I wish he would find a nice Punjabi girl to settle down with. I know several from good families, but he outright refuses to meet them."

"John doesn't like Kulvinder's girlfriend much." Mum flattens the pleats in a nightgown she's worn for days.

"I never said that," I object.

"You didn't have to, sweetheart," Mum replies.

Mrs. Sharma tops up Mum's tea and pushes a plate of sweets towards me. "Kulvinder's been impossible since he got rid of his turban. And now that this girl has come along, he's lost his senses. The boy spends money like most people flush paper down the toilet. Spend, spend, spend. Chanel this. Calvin that. It's too much."

"I said Erica's a handful," I interrupt. "I never said I didn't like her."

"If I don't give him the money, he steals from the restaurant. Can you imagine? He takes cash out of the register and denies he had anything to do with it."

As much as I dislike Kulvinder right now, I realize this talk is a parent thing. Full of wild speculation and high-wire theatrics. If I weren't around, they'd be tearing into my ass about something. Kulvinder is a lot of things, but he isn't a thief.

Even so, I'm grateful for Mrs. Sharma's company. She's one of the few people who won't treat Mum as if she's an invalid.

I hate it when the visit ends and we're alone.

"Mum, how are you feeling tonight?" I stand in her bedroom doorway.

"A bit tired, dear. Just tired." She speaks in a hoarse whisper. "I'm more concerned about you."

"Oh, Mum." I lie to give her something to feel good about. "No worries. I'm excellent. Never been better." Koech always coped well, and it'd please her no end if I did too. "There's been talk that I might win an academic prize. Gossip really. All-around excellence or something."

"That's wonderful, Son." She's curled in a ball at the centre of the bed and could use an invigorating stroll. "I always knew if you applied yourself . . ."

"Well, it's not official. But I'm a contender. Listen, Mum, it's stuffy in here. Why don't we go for a walk?"

"Is that nice friend of yours in contention?"

"Who?"

"The European girl. Svetlana."

"Oh, Svetlana." I don't know what else to suggest that'll get Mum on her feet. "Yes."

I could open the curtains.

"You ought to bring her around."

"Svetlana?"

"Svetlana, yes. You know how well we get on."

"It'll have to wait. Not long though. Right now she's busy rehearsing for her play. You should see her." I don't have the heart to say we aren't together anymore. "They've got her wearing period costumes. You know, pioneer dresses that go wide at the hips. It's hilarious. She tripped on her hem the first day."

"Your father likes that she's concerned about politics. He hopes it'll rub off on you."

"I'll make sure she stops by in a couple of weeks."

"I understand."

"Listen, Mum, do you need anything?" I'm out of conversation. "I've got homework to get to."

"Not right now, Son." She stares at the ceiling. "My stomach is cramping, my chest aches, and I don't have the

energy to do anything." Her illness makes me uncomfortable.
"I wish I could use the time to read. I used to love history not
so long ago. It was my best subject at school. I enjoyed it so
much I even started documenting stories. They weren't elaborate. Just memories elders had about more traditional times.
But with boys to raise . . . now all I think about is the state of
the kitchen cupboards. There's so much dust to get rid of.
Eating off dusty plates isn't healthy for either you or your dad."

"Shush," I say. "Shusssh."

I should do much more. Sit down at the foot of her bed and
regale her with anti-Kulvinderisms. Rub her feet. Fluff up her
pillows. Fetch her a piping hot water-bottle. But . . . I can't get
my well-conditioned legs to close that space between her
illness and the doorway.

After a couple of minutes I back into my room.

What's wrong with me?

I pick up a *Runners World* magazine. There are photographs
of shoes with springy heels and padded arch supports.

I can't concentrate.

Why can't I get over this hump?

"Listen, we're just friends anyway." Jesus. What a stupid
thing to say to her after her father went buck wild with the bat.

I should have threatened to burn the bastard with cigarettes.

My skin fits loosely over my body, and I'm disgusted with
myself.

I go to the can and find a razor. Put it down on the sink.
Pull up the sleeve of my sweater. Run a finger along my
triceps. Then pick up the blade again.

I'm nervous. I don't want to cut myself. I don't.

I put the razor down and sit on the edge of the bathtub.

There's a bottle of mouthwash on a shelf beside the mirror. I unscrew the top and knock back a few swigs.

It burns going down, and I wait for the buzz. Then I replace Dad's razor in his kit before lying down on the floor in my room.

Slow jams play on a compilation tape made for a night of serious grinding.

I find a thesaurus, plop myself down in front of the type-writer, adjust the ribbon to red and draft a letter.

As I write, "It's A Man's World" (James Brown, *Live in New York*) never sounded so good.

Amor Mio,

You're a distant and remote land, and I'm the brooding sea. I stare, lost in the chaos of lips I yearn to search with a kiss.

Dare I wish your mouth would yield to mine? Will you please realign this tide out of sync with its moon?

You see, it isn't supposed to be like this. Your father doesn't have the right. Nobody has the right. I'm not supposed to heap words, like indigent refugees, at your border.

Svetlana, you alone make my heart chakra twinge like guitar strings attacked by the bow of a cello.

Besos,

Leeds

The tone is arty, hip and bizarre enough for her to appreciate. I sprinkle the note with Mum's perfume.

In the morning I wake up at 5:30, do high knee lifts in the pool at six, work the stationary bike half an hour later and finish with some free weights. Obviously it isn't the same as banging heads with Kulvinder. Nevertheless, I push my body until my muscles can't give anymore.

Our first outdoor meet is in April, and university deadlines are in August.

I definitely won't be going to Washington State. Most of the Kenyan runners who went there ran longer distances, and I have no intention of moving up to the five. It's difficult enough doing what it takes to run a decent half-mile.

Sam has a contact in Villanova, and the calendar for Oregon offers courses in Africa and the African Diaspora. These are my top choices.

At school I slip Svetlana's note into her locker.

When I finally see her, she beats a hasty retreat. Or at least, it's the only way to explain what happens. She pulls into Math after I get there, rushes out when the bell rings, and she makes herself scarce at recess.

It's hardly the reaction I expected. I'd figured more her ripping off my boxers in the girls' locker room.

I swallow my pride and get Kulvinder to talk to her.

"What's her problem?" I hobble on crutches down the hallway after school.

"She's freaked is all," he replies.

"Were those her exact words?"

"Not exactly, dog. It's what I got from what she said."

"Well, what exactly did she say?"

"You've got to understand, she's in a tough position. She's from Eastern Europe, and they've got all that father-daughter Electra-complex shit between them."

He's walking too fast. "You're not telling me what she said."

"Forget what she said," he replies. "Forget her. Erica's got a friend. Jackie. Nice knockers. First year. I could hook you up."

I speed up, and the crutches hurt my armpits. "There's something you're not telling me."

He stops at the front door. "Move on, mate. Move on."

4

Thank God. I land myself a weekend job as a clerk at Barney's Furniture Warehouse. I've given up cutting myself, but the cravings are strong. Work is a distraction. It helps me focus on getting through the day one task at a time.

I work alone, pulling folders, sorting through documents and replacing them in file cabinets. It keeps my hands occupied.

The isolation's also brilliant because I don't get caught up in office politics. There's no approaching the supervisor, Ms. Anne Granger, MBA, to say how so-and-so never cleans his coffee mug.

I like Ms. Granger, MBA. Even if she's a frumpy beanpole with hair like an upturned bird's nest. It doesn't seem to matter that she prides herself on her ability to figure people out at first glance, like she knows them better than they know themselves.

"Oh, my brother-in-law says he's going to the Olympics," she says at our first meeting. "Been saying it for years. He'll probably keep saying it until someone comes along and gives him a good kick in the keister. Pardon my French. He acts like swimming is all there is. But that's just an excuse for not getting on with his life. Anyhoo, what did you say you run again?"

I don't object. I get to work six-hour shifts two days a week. The pay is good, and air conditioning makes the place far more comfortable than a kitchen.

I continue my regimen at the pool, although it takes more time than I'd anticipated.

There's travel time twice a day, and the workouts get longer and longer. They're broken down into segments—pool time, stationary bike and weights—with each increasing in level of difficulty with the passing days. Sam adds treading water in the deep end and makes me do quick intervals on the bicycle. The weights also get heavier, and the repetitions increase.

In order to make the schedule work, I eat on the go, do my homework at recess or on the bus and don't go out any more.

It's exhausting. But I don't want to fall behind the others. Not like Vivian, who refuses to admit it.

"I can train through this," she says. "I just gotta run on soft surfaces is all."

One positive is that Sam and I talk more, mostly about Kenyan athletes and their contribution to the sport. He surprises me with his knowledge of obscure runners such as Richard Juma. The 10 000-metre specialist retired for eight years to fulfil his father's desire to see him get hitched and raise a brood. However, when Juma returned to competition, he set a Kenyan record of 27.57.0 when he finished third at the 'seventy-four Commonwealth Games.

Dad and I keep such irregular hours that it takes seven days before the entire family is together again.

We sit in front of the television and watch the weather girl flash her teeth throughout her report.

"Ow." My right calf cramps. "Ouch."

"What?" Dad asks.

"Cramp."

"Where?"

I point it out. He leans forward and rubs a knot in the belly of my calf.

Dad's been setting the tone since Mum got sick. Bright. Bubbly. Enthusiastic. All while we collectively remain mute about *it*, the illness having become an *it*. A word we use to avoid saying arteriosclerosis, as if naming the disease makes *it* less manageable, more overwhelming.

But, despite our silence, *it* becomes increasingly difficult to avoid. There *it* is in a pamphlet about heart disease on the coffee table. Or else *it* appears among the potted plants in the room. Right there where the aloe vera leaves have begun to wilt.

"I think it's important that we move away from here." Lately he's been talking about different neighbourhoods. "There are other places to live. Other possibilities."

"*David Letterman* is about to start," I announce.

"We ought to start our own business." He places my leg back on the coffee table. "There are all sorts of opportunities in this country." He's been listening to self-help quacks on pricey audio tapes purchased during a recent binge. "We could start our own organization. Focus on Africa. There are still valid needs in so many places. We could approach some of my old colleagues about this. Of course, finding funding will be tricky. But where there's a will . . ."

Mum eggs him on while he speculates about speculating on the stock market and comes up with scenarios that we can take advantage of through telemarketing. Thinks of ways we can break into retail. "Tomorrow I'm going to send for a mailing list," he says.

"Start-up money is a problem," Mum replies.

But "where there's a will . . ."

He leaves the room for a quick consultation with the tapes.

Damn. We missed Dave's opening monologue.

The following evening I emerge from a lukewarm shower and wander into the living room, where I'm greeted by Slim.

"Jesus, what happened to your hair?" It looks like he's taken a machete to his head in a sorry attempt at imitating my haircut.

"Come, I wanna show you somethin." He grabs my hand, pulls me outside and from out of the bushes hauls a large box wrapped in newspaper.

"Shouldn't you be out throwing rocks at cars or something?" I ask.

"Merry Christmas," he replies.

"It isn't Christmas yet."

"My new home is here to pick me up."

Of course, the foster home! I forgot. "Wasn't that supposed to happen at the end of the month?"

"Ma got sick," he says. "She's in the Sycotronic Ward."

"Psychiatric Ward?"

"Uhuh."

I carefully unwrap the paper.

"Damn, Slim." It's a ghetto blaster.

"I lifted it."

"That's nice of you, but you can't go around stealing shit."

"Whatch you get me?"

"Slim!"

"I didn't do nothing bad."

"Don't misunderstand me. I'm . . ."

"It's Larry's. But he ain't comin back, so I stoled it for you. Jus' don't tell Ma, okay?"

I take him inside and set him up in the kitchen with a plate of cookies. He crams a handful into his mouth.

"I'll be back in a jiffy." I go up to my room and fetch Koech's track top.

"Take good care of this," I say.

"Cool." He hugs me and runs outside to a car parked in the street.

Jugs sits in the back seat and looks the other way.

No goodbye.

When they pull away, I wave. Slim's nose is flat against the window.

My insides snap when he waves back.

I ring Svetlana at the theatre.

It's time to deal with her square on. Watching Jugs disappear like that made me think about the way Svetlana came through at the hospital, the rainy night in the hotel. How I'd got riled up over Papa and managed to mess up by not going to her with how that felt.

I'll apologize and coax her back with some Dr. Martin Luther King.

I have a dream, Svetlana. I have a dream that little black children and little white children will one day be able to . . .

Some bloke answers the phone and says she just left with Alan.

Who's Alan?

Have I already been replaced?

It takes two weeks for the swelling at my ankle to disappear, and I'm now able to get around without crutches. Managing without Svetlana will be another matter.

5

After another punishing session at the pool, Sam finally reads Vivian the riot act.

"How's the knee coming along?" he asks. She showed up but skipped the pool work.

"It ain't. I can't get rid of the swellin."

"Did I ever tell you about Moscow in 'eighty? I was dating Diane Fisher, the sprinter from Winnipeg. What a talent she was. She made the team in the one, the two and both relays. Anyway, Diane felt a twinge in her knee at a twilight meet at a high performance camp in Utah. But she didn't do much about it. I tried to tell her, pay now or pay later. I said, there's always another Games. But did she listen? Not on your life. She iced it, put a bandage on it and kept pushing. She wanted to go to the Games. That was all that mattered to her. Getting to the Games. Anyhow, we boycotted that year. It wasn't a decision I agreed with. I mean, we hadn't done anything to support the African boycott in 'seventy-six. Sport and politics weren't supposed to mix. But there we were, pulling out of

Moscow because of Afghanistan. Figure that one out. Anyway, we didn't go to the Games, and Diane had pushed her knee past the point of no return. She attempted a comeback in 'eighty-four, but the field had moved past her by then."

"What's some has-been sprinter gotta do with me?"

"Think about it."

"No fuckin way am I getting cut."

"God, you're stubborn."

"Ballsy is more like it."

"No, stubborn and foolish. You'll have to get it operated on. It's the only way we'll be able to fix the ligament damage. The truth is, even if you do have the operation, you may never run the hurdles again. Your knee won't be able to handle the pounding."

She glares at him. "I'll be cool."

"I'm just trying to save you a lot of heartache. You need to get it operated on and think about moving up to the eight. You're quick and strong. It won't be too much of a stretch for you to make the transition. Look at Jarmila Kratochvilova. Sure, some people say she was on steroids. Let 'em talk. She's got her records and her medals. If they're tainted, she knows about it. That's her private hell to deal with. The main thing is you could be that kind of runner, quick and strong. Quick over 400 metres, and strong from the hurdles. I'm from the school that says Edwin Moses in his prime could have put a scare into Coe's 800-metre record. He ran 1.44 once. Don't quote me on that. It was a rumour doing the rounds. But if he'd focused on it, there's no telling how he could have rewritten the record books. Vivian, what I'm saying here is you've got a decision to make, and you shouldn't take too much time thinking about it."

Vivian and I limp towards the bus stop together, tension between us.

"I ain't movin up to the eight. That's two motherfuckin laps. It hurts enough going around once. I ain't runnin no two motherfuckin laps."

"Sam's only . . ."

"Sam can suck my pussy. Fuck. I need a meeting. I ought to just get my ass to an AA meeting."

"Listen, Viv. Don't sweat it," I say. "These things ultimately work themselves out."

"Not today. I can't listen to anymore of that shit today. Keep it real. I put in the work. Go to my meetings. Do my steps. But where the fuck are the results? Nada. Nowhere."

"Viv."

"Get cut. What the fuck? I may as well kiss off any chance of making it to Tokyo. Move up to the eight. Has the nigga lost it? He may as well just lock me up in juvie for the next ten months."

"I don't . . ."

"Goddamnit all to hell. If I don't get a meeting, I'm gonna bust up somethin."

"Violence isn't such a good idea. You've been doing so well lately. Your curfews been lifted and . . ."

She cringes as if I've taken a paddle to her. "You ain't serious."

"Of course not. I just meant . . ."

"Well, fuck you too."

I didn't mean to sound like such a straight-laced jackass, but she makes me nervous.

"Forget I said anything. I just start jabbering away and rubbish comes flying out my mouth. Ask Kulvinder. He'll tell you. I'm half man, half imbecile. Well, maybe not quite half. More like a quarter. No, an eighth. I'm about an eighth imbecile. Inherited of course from a randy plantation owner back in the day. I've got documents to prove it. Not on me. But . . ."

She laughs. "Just shut the fuck up, okay?"

When I get home, a letter from Svetlana is waiting for me on the kitchen table.

She says there's nothing to be done. Nothing. Papa is having her followed, and she's afraid. There's nothing to do except move on.

I grab leftovers from the fridge and storm off to my room with a plate of food.

The bathroom door is ajar, and Mum stands in her underthings in front of the mirror. She pinches rolls of loose skin at her belly and jiggles hanging folds at her thighs. Tears leak from her eyes.

I creep past and climb onto my bed with my food.

I want to hug her and tell her everything will be okay. To say, as I tried to say to Vivian, "These things have a way of working themselves out." But I haven't craved cutting in a couple of weeks, and I'm afraid if I stop to speak, my insides will get muddled again.

I swallow a lump that has lodged itself in my throat.

. . . If I run the first four in fifty-five seconds, all I have to do is come back in fifty-four. Even splits. Twenty-seven seconds over . . .

6

The injury isn't as severe as the doctor originally thought, and I'm doing dry-land workouts again. The break doesn't seem to have hurt me. Quite the opposite: my legs are stronger than they've ever been. Sure, there's a little rust, but otherwise I'm running better than before.

The change helps me keep from obsessing about Svetlana.

I'm averaging five-minute miles on my quicker long runs and am doing up to eighty miles a week.

The picture of Kulvinder kicking my butt in Calgary is now tacked onto my headboard. It's an image I'll take down only when I can replace it with one in which the results are reversed.

My goal is to run 1.46.3. That was Koech's personal best.

1.46.3.

Not a problem if I get fit enough to put together back-to-back fifty-three-second quarters.

Thankfully, my body seems to be filling out. There are ripples in the right places—at my hamstrings, on my stomach and even above my quadriceps on my upper thighs. My muscles are a delight to behold when I flex naked in front of the bathroom mirror, a neatly shorn head adding to the viewing pleasure.

I weigh a hundred and fifty pounds, up ten from the summer.

Sam doesn't know it, but I've begun fitting in extra work, little things to give me an edge.

I rummage through my closet for Koech's army boots. With indelible ink I write "1.46.3" under their protruding tongues and train in the clunkers on the days I run on my own.

When we do intervals, I hold my breath. Just sucking it up for as long as possible. It's what Cruz did the year he dismantled the field in L.A.

I've also taken to sneaking into the weight room at the Community Centre after workouts.

Edwin Moses didn't eat red meat very often. A move I make to get my body fat percentage down. I'd like to be closer to four percent and get rid of the extra three percent I'm lugging around.

My resting pulse rate is forty-eight on most days; pretty good considering Henry Rono's wasn't much lower than that in his heyday.

Sam and I talk on the phone at least twice a week. We go over our plans, resting pulse rates, minor aches, mental visualization and weight.

I feel world-class. Coe had his father, Snell had Lydiard, and I have Sam.

Of course, I'm careful to keep much of this stuff from Kulvinder. Not that he gives a fig. He's so wrapped up in Erica, I can't remember the last time he took his head out of his ass.

He's already begun reneging on our pledge to go to the States.

"Erica says it's a meat-grinder down there. Your season starts in the fall with cross-country, then there are meets indoors, and then you've got to race outside. By the time N.C.A.A.'s roll around in May, your legs are toast, and there's still three more months of the track season to go."

"What are you saying?"

"Nothing. It's just something to think about. They're really into a whole-team concept. Not only do you have your own races to run, but there are relays as well. It's all about points and winning championships for the school."

"So you don't want to go?"

"I'm not saying that. I'm just thinking long-term. You can't tell people who are paying your way that you're concerned about burnout. They'll toss you out on your ear."

"This is what Erica tells you?"

"Yeah. That's why she didn't go to Stanford. She figured she'd stay with Sam and work on building something long-term. There's a European circuit that offers prize money, and it makes more sense to peak for that. Nobody remembers who won the N.C.A.A.'s. No one. Why not be smart and build a career around the World Championships and the Olympics?"

I don't like what I'm hearing.

It wouldn't surprise me if the wanker is stealing from his Mum to keep Erica eating in four-star restaurants.

Dumb pillock.

Just wait till we get outdoors. I'll burn it up all the way to Villanova. Kulvinder won't know what hit him.

Mum starts vomiting again the day thick packages arrive in the mail.

Dr. Olsen is away on holiday. So she ends up seeing his substitute, a young woman named Dr. Weber.

"So there she was, asking me all kinds of questions." Mum says on her return. "'Are you currently taking any medications? Any allergies?' I didn't like the way she went on. Couldn't she just check the file?"

"She seemed so young and inexperienced," Dad interjects. "So I explained it all to her."

"That was when she told us that I'd been misdiagnosed."

"Misdiagnosed! Can you believe that, Son? After all your mother's been through."

"But what about all that stuff about plaque build-up?" I ask.

"I never had an angiogram," Mum says. "You can't be definitively diagnosed with arteriosclerosis without an angiogram. So she's going to do a different round of tests."

She starts to casually open the thick envelopes. The letters guarantee that if we follow their money-making program—to which George Thomas of Akron, Ohio, or Sally Reeves of Boston, Massachusetts, owe their success—we will earn millions.

It's a confusing time. I have no idea what's going on. First Mum is at death's door. Then I find out it may all have been a mistake. Now we're sitting around on pins and needles as we wait for news about her latest batch of blood tests.

I call Svetlana and hang up after the first ring. Then I track her down in the hallway, but we wind up having a polite and disconnected chat. How's acting? Fine. Track? Good.

The weather's been mild for this time of year. Blah, blah. I contemplate taking another beating from Papa to prove the sincerity of my feelings.

In the end it seems smarter to let go. My presence only increases her suffering.

What choice do I have?

I start making all sorts of stupid blunders at work. On Tuesday I file the A's with the C's. On Thursday folders to be sorted and placed in the IN box I put into the OUT box. This leads to my first warning from Ms. Granger, MBA, on Friday.

"I realize you're preparing for—quote—the Nationals—unquote. But this is no excuse for negligence at work. I've been informed that on top of your sloppy filing, you haven't been refilling the photocopier with paper. I'm disappointed, John. I really thought you might take advantage of this opportunity. A reference from our office could open a lot of doors for someone of your, uh, background. Try to make sure you don't give me an occasion to revisit this conversation. Do we understand each other?"

Yes, I'm letting down the side. Not so much the other members of the office team as the entire black race.

7

The call from Vivian comes as Sam pulls into the driveway to pick me up for a workout on a cross-country course out of town.

"Vivian just phoned," I say, climbing into an old beat-up truck he's recently salvaged from an auction. "She sounds shaken. She wants to know if we can go over to the group home right away."

"When it rains, it certainly pours."

His truck is a wreck. The glove compartment is held in place by twine. The floor beneath my feet is rusted through, and the road peeps up from a gaping hole. "She's an old truck. But has a good engine. I just got the transmission fixed."

The seatbelt's caked in mud, and I can't get it to lock around my waist. "Is she going to make it to practice?"

"We'll find out soon enough." He changes gears to the sound of a choke mixing with a sputter.

I'm not much of a car person. It's one of those things I can't explain. Irrational, but somehow cars are connected to how I figure my life will end.

"Does this kind of thing happen much?" I babble.

"Transmission failure?"

"No. Drama with your athletes."

"Often enough."

I hope Vivian hasn't stuck a fork in someone's eye.

We make a quick left followed by a long right and pull up at a home surrounded by cop cars. We hustle up the front steps and walk through an empty sitting room into the kitchen.

Sam is out of breath. He must be carrying six inches of blubber around his waist.

A woman talks on the phone, and I can see a group of cops through a window behind her. Laden with flashlights, guns and notepads, they mill around a shed.

A kid with a ponytail stumbles into the kitchen as he wipes sleep from his eyes. "What the fuck?" He stifles a yawn.

"Clive, go and get dressed," the woman says, hanging up the phone. "We'll talk about it in the car on the way to breakfast. Just go get dressed."

"I didn't do nothing."

"Nobody said you did. Just get dressed."

"Sorry about the chaos, Sam," the woman says. "It's been quite a morning."

Vivian interrupts her. "I need to get the hell out. Get me the hell out of this hole."

Vivian tries to talk once we're in the car, but everything that comes out of her mouth is a sob.

"It's okay," says Sam, offering her his cup of coffee. "You don't have to say anything. Why don't you skip the workout today? I'll drop you off at my place. You can stay there as long as you need. I have to go up to Abbottsford to let the others know that I'm cancelling practice. But Leeds can stay with you until I get back."

Kioko stirs soup in a saucepan on the stove. "You ought to get something into your stomach, Vivian," she says.

"I could use a shot a tequila."

"Kioko probably has some ginseng extract stashed away someplace. Would that do?"

I used to think Viv was all prickles and no soft centre. But I was wrong.

"Today's been fuckin nuts."

"What happened, sweetie?"

She looks down at her feet. "I'm in the shed trying to find a hammer to hang a couple of pictures. But the light switch is buggin. Nada. After my eyes adjust I see what I figure is the hammer on a table. But as I reach for it, I knock a bag of nails to the floor." She stops to gather herself. "Which is when I see the girl." She looks as if she's going to cry. "I figure she's just coppin zzz's. So I give her a shake. But she doesn't move." Kioko reaches for her hand while I stand to stir the bubbling soup.

"You've got to find another place to live," Kioko says.

"Those fuckin pigs kept asking me all kinds of dumb-ass questions. Then I had to write everything down." I place a bowl of soup in front of her.

"We've got to get you out of there," Kioko says.

"It's my third goddamned placement in two years. I don't want to go to another group home." Her eyes redden. "I've

gotta get semi-independent living next month. I can't handle
that shit hole."

Vivian moves in with Sam and Kioko that day. There will
be bureaucratic hassles to deal with, but nothing insurmount-
able. They'll talk to her probation officer about being her
guardians, and she'll live in their basement until they manage
to fix up the garage.

When I get home, there's a turquoise Volkswagen van
parked out front. A white man with blonde dreds carries
boxes into the apartment upstairs.

"Guidance," he says.

"Respect," I reply.

I don't like him already.

To be honest, I half-hoped Jugs and the little squirt would
reappear and we could all start over.

8

final exams are in two days, but I can't seem to concentrate on anything for more than a minute and a half.

I stare at page 132 of my math text.

Algorithms!

I close the book and re-examine the letter sent by Svetlana.

It's tough to let go. A thought that heightens the resentment I feel for Kulvinder's thing with Erica.

I mean, Erica used to be kind of cool. Sure, the hen-pecking got on my nerves, but she was basically all right. However, ever since they got into all that private gossiping, he just drifted away. Now he's a Chablis-drinking and matching-dish-towel-set-buying squit.

Not that I envy her and desire to fondle his buttocks or stick gerbils up his ass. Nothing like that.

It's just . . .

I bury my troubles in the only place I have left to go: farting around with Vivian.

"What a messed up world we live in," I say while we wait for a bus.

"I'd toss every freaking dope dealer into a pit full of dead junkies if I was running things," she replies.

It's one of our best conversations to date. We riff on our plans to change the world. Everyone would have the same amount of money. There wouldn't be any pigs. Politicians would have to mud wrestle in order to settle their beefs. Stupid stuff like that.

I'm pretty randy by the time we get through the bit about mud wrestling. All I can think of is leaning in, the big lip-to-lip. Her tongue hip to my tip.

By the time my brain has finished its introductory argument in defense of the motion to kiss . . . "My bus," she says.

I suck in my gut, pucker up and make my move. But she turns away, and my meaty chops collide with her upper cheekbone.

9

It takes four days before Dr. Weber discovers the source of Mum's illness.

It turns out that she has pinched a nerve in her chest, and the vomiting is caused by an allergy to nuts.

I thought I'd be relieved. But I feel an odd remoteness, a strange sense of joylessness. There is no touching feel-good moment. No searching conversations in which we talk of all the love in the room.

We've caught a break and are being rushed by circumstances to move on. Get ahead. Be on top of things in case anything bad is to befall the Pacific West Coast settlement of the Kipligat clan again.

Mum pulls out a purple pouch I've never seen before, sprinkles a bag of red soil onto the altar and pours drops from a vial of brown river water. Then she chants to the Knowledge Holders in rhythms I've never heard before.

The next afternoon, after an outing with Mrs. Sharma, Mum appears with two thousand five hundred dollars.

"We can't accept her money," Dad says.

"We can and we will." Mum winks at me.

The Knowledge Holders have provided the . . . knowledge, and Dad kicks it up a gear.

"Car alarms," he says as he produces a newspaper article chronicling the changing demographics in the Lower Mainland. "The city is growing, which means that the crime rates are going to go up. Therefore, security will be an issue. If we can start supplying quality alarm systems, we'll be on our way."

It isn't a bad idea. Who can't use a quality anti-theft device?

There's a quote from Alexander Graham Bell that Sam recently threw into his latest sermon to the troops. It goes something like, "What this power is I cannot say; all I know is that it exists, and it becomes available only when a man is in that state of mind in which he wants something and is fully determined not to quit until he finds it." The gender-unfriendly language would get Svetlana in a snit. But the basic message is apt.

Armed with the power of positive thinking and a big thumbs-up from the audio tapes, Dad makes a deal with Mr. Chen to pay rent two weeks late and hands in his notice at the high school.

Emboldened by her visit with the Knowledge Holders, Mum sends away for a book with a list of companies that sell alarms wholesale. Then they get busy looking through catalogues, ordering goods and pulling together an advertising package. They will give the business their full attention.

"I feel very good about this," Mum comments as her energy level increases. "The overhead is low, and with Christmas just around the corner the return should be high."

"Not 'should,'" Dad says, sending away for lists of both residential and business addresses to which to mail their advertising package. "'Will.' The return will be high."

It's like the old days.

Running is going well. We're out of school for Christmas break and I press Kulvinder on my better days. Although, somewhere in the back of my mind, I still worry that my ankle will give out like a punctured tire.

Practices tend to be heavy on the long intervals. Lots of repeat 3000's. This work is geared towards building stamina. So it isn't as if I'm not busting my butt.

"We're preparing to run two races in Montreal," Sam says. "We want to be fit enough to get through the heats and still have something left for the final." He's big on proceeding as if our selection to the team is certain. "Remember, 'on the way to one's beloved, there are no hills.'"

I've mailed out my application package to Villanova but have given up on Oregon. I can't afford to apply to both. No problem, though. Sydney Maree, the South African miler, went to Villanova.

Unfortunately, Kulvinder still hasn't sent his in. He's got a new set of goals worked out with Erica.

Vivian half-heartedly pecks away at a program of ultrasound treatments, deep-tissue massage and pool workouts. But nothing gets rid of the swelling.

It's clear she's falling well behind the rest of us, and I feel for her.

It's also obvious she's only interested in friendship.

"I been with Will since I was thirteen," she says. "Man, the nigga's crazy. You know, got me into b'n e's, petty bullshit like that. Got paid too. But that was after I split from home."

I try to downplay my shock. "You left home when you were thirteen!"

"Fuck, yeah. Moms' had lung cancer, 'n I wasn't gonna be no nurse maid to her. The bitch never paid *me* no mind."

"Thirteen!"

"Hey, I ain't fishin for a pity party," she says.

"Oh, no," I stammer. "I don't feel sorry for you." Not true. "I mean . . . I don't know what I mean."

She laughs. "It's okay, Negro. It's just what is. I don't sit around gettin hot about shit I can't change. Pops split on Moms when she got pregnant with me. Moms is sick. I ain't gonna cry about it. It's just what is."

"Don't you miss having some kind of family? You know, grandparents. Something."

"Hey, fuck or be fucked. It ain't personal. Moms split on her folks when she was fourteen. She wasn't gonna spend her life in no ghetto in L.A. Nothing personal. I left 'cause I had to go. Since then Will's been family. Now even that's headin for the exits. But that's just the way it go."

I haven't sussed out all the details, but their relationship is messed.

For instance, they have a cat he looks after because Vivian wasn't allowed a pet in the group home. But whenever they fight, he threatens to break its neck if he doesn't get his way.

Man, I need to keep my distance. I'd be a clod to get drawn into the middle of that drama; I ought to stay focused on the scholarship.

God, I miss Svetlana.

On Christmas Day we sleep in. Then Mum and Dad get to work on organizing the business while I go for a quick ten-miler.

The rest of the day is uneventful. We have ham and mashed potatoes with peas for dinner. Then Mum, Dad and I huddle around the telly and watch *The Wizard of Oz*.

10

All forward momentum comes to an abrupt halt at the end of January.

The culprit this time is money or, at least, the flow of money. It's going out a hell of a lot faster than it's coming in.

The root of the problem is our first big investment. A car.

Dad figured our lives would be far less complicated if we bought one. So he and Mum scoured a number of dealerships before settling on a second-hand Honda Accord.

It wouldn't have been a problem if we hadn't run into a number of mechanical bung-ups the week after the purchase. The car's transmission started acting up, and it soon became evident that the radiator would also have to be replaced.

"Not to worry," Mum says. "Money's on the way. The business will be off the ground by the middle of next month."

So we head off the first potential crisis. Dad strikes a bargain with the slumlord. We'll pay February's rent two weeks late.

They dive headlong into getting the business off the ground as quickly as possible. It's another expensive endeavour. It costs to register and apply for a licence. The graphic designer bilks them with an exorbitant fee, and the minimum print run of the advertising material is much larger than they want.

There are also business cards, letterheads and mail-outs to deal with. The whole thing sets them back so much that we're now reliant on the money I bring home from the filing job.

"We're right where we ought to be," Dad says as stock piles up in the living room. It's merchandise just itching to be shipped. Boxes full of boxes containing top-quality car alarms. All of them primed and ready to make the growing population of the Lower Mainland rest easy in their sleep.

Response is slow, an order here, another there. But no worries, more from the book of Sam: "Image creates desire. You will what you imagine."

So we imagine. We envision the mailbox filling up with orders and banish all negative thoughts from our minds.

"Let's turn our attention to the phones," Mum says. "We can start ringing people up at noon and go until eight o'clock in the evening."

I help out when I can, although I turn out to be something of a liability. I hate interrupting folks who've just sat down to a soap or are in the middle of a spirited squabble. It seems rude, and I'm humbled when they politely tell me to fuck off.

I don't let any of this interfere with my training, though. Not at all: I'm so motivated it hurts. Nothing is going to make me miss a workout this month.

I still fight daily not to cut myself, but at least I'm on the way to my first consistent stretch at ninety miles a week. All I need to do is hang in there until the beginning of March, and it'll be four solid weeks.

On occasion I watch videotapes with Sam, Kiki and Vivian. Kiki turns out to be real funny. She always gets Sam to admit to the boneheaded things he did as an athlete. Like the time he got caught toilet-papering the dorms of Canada's female athletes during the 'seventy-eight Commonwealth Games. It took the intervention of the team captain to stop the coaches from sending him home.

The three of them are like a second family, and with their urging I start to talk more about Nairobi. When I finally tell them about Koech's disappearance, they're moved. Both Sam and Kiki choke up, and Vivian treats me with a new-found respect.

One night I return from Sam's to find Dad talking Mr. Chen into another extension on the rent. Standing in the doorway, he explains about the unexpected expenses and how things are certain to pick up. Then he throws in a car alarm for good measure.

"I have mortgage to pay. You understand." The stingy bugger isn't having it. "If I don't see rent by end of business day, I take you to court. Uh."

"We've been good tenants for two years," Dad says. "Never once have we been late on the rent."

"I have three buildings," Mr. Chen replies. "No, four buildings. Two are behind on rent, Mr. Kipligat. I make no exception. You understand. Uh."

"Two years, Mr. Chen," Dad repeats.

"One couple has baby girl. They split up. This is not my problem. Mortgage is my problem."

Dad starts to shout, "Take us to court then."

I've been listening from the kitchen, and I make a quick exit to my bedroom.

After Mr. Chen leaves, I can hear Mum try to smooth things over with Dad. "I can pick up some hours doing childcare," she suggests. "The agency is always short-staffed at this time of year."

"No, Gladys," he says. "The telephone could ring at any time with an order. Nothing is impossible."

The notice comes in the mail the following morning. We have until March first to pay two months rent, or else.

"Evicted!" Dad laughs. "He can't just throw us out in the streets."

"Come on, Dad."

"Ahab, we've tried. Things haven't worked as we hoped." She waters plants and pulls off the dead leaves. "We can regroup and try again in six months."

"Let him come and throw us into the streets," Dad rages. "Just let him come."

There's no debating the matter. Dad decides we're not going anywhere. He'll barricade the doors. Engage in hand-to-hand combat. Nobody, but nobody, is going to kick us out of our home.

I get my ninety miles in despite all the distractions.

Any athlete worth their salt isn't taking time off just because their personal life's a mess. Sam says, "Every situation, properly perceived, is an opportunity."

We still have no place to go by the thirtieth. Dad has dug his heels in, and he isn't going to budge.

"In two years we haven't been late with a cheque. Even when Gladys was ill, the man got his money on the first of the month." Dad walks around pointing at different fixtures. "Look at this light in the hallway. We put that in at our expense. Not to mention the time we had to pay for new plumbing in the bathroom." He's been talking like this for days. "You know what, I'll go to the newspapers if it comes down to it."

The newspapers!

"Talk to him, Mum," I plead.

"Ahab, there are certain realities we have to face." She loops an arm into his.

"This isn't right," Dad says. "Who does that man think painted his place? Who paid for it? People must be made aware of how corrupt this all is."

I lose my composure. "I'm moving."

Dad shakes Mum loose and gets in my face. "I'm still your father." He wags a finger. "If I say we're going to the papers, that's what we'll do."

I envision our family on the front page of that gossip rag, *The Province*. The write-up is on page three, next to the smiling bikini-clad "Sunshine Girl."

Refugees Cry Foul

Ahab Kipligat and his family are being evicted from 1100 Stamp St. Mr. Kipligat claims that he is being wrongfully removed from said premises due to racism.

"We've been good tenants for two years," he said. "Now we are being thrown out into the street like animals. Animals!"

The landlord has declined to comment. He did not answer calls from *The Province*.

Jim Benning is advocating on the family's behalf. "What we have here is clearly a contravention of Article six of the Human Rights Code. There is a precedent in Collins versus Abdallah. 1976. Yes, it's a law that is subject to interpretation, but the accused and I are willing to argue our case in the Supreme Court. Such egregious violations of human rights must be remedied."

John "Leeds" Kipligat, the son of the co-accused, was unwilling to discuss the matter.

"I'm not at liberty to talk about the case until it has run its course through the system," he said.

A spokesperson for the New Democratic Party insisted that the status of refugees remains a priority. "Our record on immigration speaks for itself. We are the only party to propose the selection of a task force, made up of community leaders, with a clear mandate to fact-find on the plight of refugees."

I shout a bunch of incoherent obscenities and tear out of the apartment in search of Vivian.

When I walk into her room at Sam's place, I find her conked out on her bed with an open bottle of codeine beside her head.

I shake her.

"Vivian. Can you hear me?"

"Whaaa?"

"Viv, can you hear me?"

"Of course I can, nigga. You're yellin in my ear."

"How many fingers am I holding up?"

"Have you lost your fuckin mind?"

"You're not trying to . . . you know, are you?"

"Off myself?"

"I just . . ."

"I ain't killin myself."

"Well, you've been under a lot of pressure lately and I thought . . . Well, I thought . . ."

"We're not having this conversation. And stop lookin at me like that. I'm doin good. So get off my back."

I pick up the bottle of codeine. "Is this a good idea? I mean with your history and all."

"It's for the knee." She snatches it back. "What a busy mind you got."

I've calmed down by the time I get home. I need to focus. We'll be doing the final workout of a ninety-mile-a-week cycle tomorrow.

Dad ignores me. "Gladys, have you seen the receipts for July and August rents?"

"They should be in with the others," Mum yells from where she kneels at her altar.

I was going to apologize. But fuck it, I go to bed.

It's 9:30 on a Friday night, and I want to get some decent sleep. It's one of the many sacrifices I'm willing to make before a well-earned two-week break.

We start on the hill. Four sets of five 200's at race pace, with a jog-back recovery between each and a walk-back recovery between each set.

Kulvinder usually comes after me early. Throwing everything at me until I crack.

Not today, though. I stay with him through the first two sets. Just hanging off his shoulder until the final thirty, then moving up beside him and staying there till the finish.

When I catch him peeking over his shoulder on the ninth one, I sense that he's in trouble.

Serves the bastard right for doing whatever the hell Erica had him doing last night. Sniffing scented candles while bathing in aromatic bath oils. Tossing back bottles of wine imported from the south of France. Making love.

When the third set gets under way, I pounce, peeling out front and staying there for the first 150. Then backing off slightly before pouring it on again over the final twenty.

Give him credit, though. He won't let me go, battling with me to the finish on each one.

He's weakening by the thirteenth two. I can hear it in the way his feet drag during the jog downhill. The poor sod's trying to buy time on the recovery.

During the last set I accelerate from fifty metres out. Pressing with everything I've got, my feet clawing at the tarmac.

He stays with me for the first two. Then he breaks.

The distance between us is up to three metres by the last one.

I don't say anything when we walk over to the track to finish up with two sets of four 300's. I'm thinking about the next one. I'm thinking, get out hard and don't let up, the larger the gap between us at the end of each interval, the better.

My lead stretches out further with each repetition, and even Erica is starting to pinch his heels.

After the last one I turn and wait for him at the finish, my hands on my hips. Forty metres later he falls to his knees at the side of the track.

I'm hurting, but I won't bend over to catch my breath. Not on your life. What matters most is that he thinks it was a walk in the park for me.

"Good work, Leeds," he finally says, getting back on his feet. "Good work."

"You too," I reply.

Sam has us do a strength circuit afterwards. Lots of push-ups, sit-ups, high knee lifts and tuck jumps. I'm unconscious. I don't feel a thing. He could make us do ten more hills afterwards, and I wouldn't give a shit.

After I warm down, Sam takes me aside. "You still have a tendency to cock your head to the side when you hit full speed," he says. "Don't cock your head."

11

Mum and I move into Pembroke Estates, a town house complex close to a glass factory, by March third. We have no choice but to leave Dad behind. He has locked himself into the old place, armed with his audio tapes.

"I'm not going anywhere," he says. "As God is my witness, I'll stay until I'm forcibly removed by the police."

"Could you shove over, Ahab?" Mum says. "I need to pack that blanket you're sitting on."

There are good things about the new place. The hot water works, although it sometimes comes out of the taps a little brown. Our windows are intact, even though several of them don't close all the way, and we have control of the thermostat.

"Don't worry about your father," Mum says, during a commercial break on *N.Y.P.D. Blue*. "He'll come around."

"I couldn't care less," I lie.

She puts an arm around me. "You're a lot like him, pumpkin. Full of fanciful ideas." She laughs. "Even if it means sitting in a drafty apartment without hot water or heat."

I let that go. There's bugger-all to argue in my defense.

I stare at the telly.

I'm woken up at seven in the morning by smashing glass.

My ankle is stiff when I walk to the window. I look outside and see workers chucking huge plates of glass into a large bin.

I open up a dresser drawer, find the picture of Kulvinder beating me in Calgary and tack it back onto my headboard. Then I get back into bed, put the pillow over my head and try to sleep in.

APRIL:
Homestretch

7

Out ahead of Kulvinder I leap over a fallen tree trunk. My feet slip as I land in a trail of loose bark. I push past a small lake full of water lilies before pressing towards the bench we use as a finish line.

Flick. Turn over. Flick. Flick. Stay up on your toes. Flick. Drive from the ankle. Flick, one last surge. Flick. Flick.

Kulvinder struggles in five seconds later. His legs gave out on him on the eighth loop.

Vigorously, a dog shakes itself after stepping out of the water, and we set out on a warm-down jog.

Kicking Kulvinder's ass hasn't been satisfying. He's more distant than ever.

I've put the boot to him for a couple of weeks now. No mercy. Just grabbing him by the scruff and rubbing his nose in it. It's nothing too nasty, though. I'm just sleazily upbeat, with a hearty dose of Pollyanna.

"You okay?" I ask.

"What's with the third degree? Course I'm okay. You?"

April 209

"Yeah. The fifth one was a little hairy. But I seem to be recovering quicker than usual."

Neither one of us hears the van until it's too late.

"Yahoooooooo." Spit. Spit. "Yahoooooooo. Yahoooooooo." Spit. Spit. Spit.

Then the fuckers peel away with a pair of butt cheeks pressed up against a window.

"Great." Kulvinder says, wiping snot from his forehead. "This piece of shit day couldn't get any worse."

"Sod it." I clean up with my T-shirt. "They'll be mooning their way to nowhere when we're sitting pretty on a national team."

If he weren't so zapped, he'd have wrung my neck. Who could blame him? Even getting hawked on by a bunch of yahoos doesn't faze me.

I stare at the telly and try to decide how future nastiness between Kulvinder and me should be handled in the press. The prying hacks.

The doorbell interrupts me.

It's Erica. She's bawling, and her bottom lip is split open.

"He clocked me," she blurts. "He fucking clocked me."

I steer her to the sofa, put the kettle on and fetch her a cloth dipped in cold water.

"I'd made us a nice dinner, red snapper, broccoli and a side of Greek salad. I even picked up a fresh loaf of rye from Uprising Bakery. But did he notice? Not in the least. He was all worked up about getting spit on. Then he got stupid. 'I'm fine. Nothing's the matter. Forget it.' All that petty bull I don't have time for." She talks quickly. "So I thought, he's an adult. If he's got something to say ... and I began folding the clothes he was shedding all over the apartment, which I'd just finished tidying up. 'Don't treat me like an invalid,' he yelled, then he grabbed them from me and scattered them around the room." She sniffles. "I couldn't believe it. He was ranting, flinging his clothes all over the place, and when I tried to stop him, he clocked me."

"Hey, c'mon Erica. Don't cry." I try to soften my tone. But I still sound like a sergeant major handing out marching orders. "Don't cry."

"I was going to make a pecan pie for dessert. Can you believe it? I was going to make him a pecan pie."

"Listen. Do you want some tea? I've got some water boiling on the stove."

"Only if you have chamomile."

I hide out in the kitchen, where I try to collect my thoughts. I decide to ring up Vivian. Erica will have to stay with her while I get Kulvinder sorted out.

"What's with you people?" Vivian says. She sounds spacey. "Will and I get in fist fights all the time." Will, the cat-strangler. "I'm surprised Kulvinder didn't pop the pushy Kitsilano bitch earlier."

"Just pick her up, Viv."

I stick a cup of watered-down black tea into Erica's mitts, and we wait for Vivian.

"Does Kulvinder ever talk to you about his dad?"

"Not really. No."

She scratches her legs. "He doesn't have to take on the world alone, you know."

"Uhuh."

"You don't like me much, do you?"

"Not true."

She has a sip from her cup. "Wow. This isn't bad tea. What brand is it?"

Kulvinder and I drink cups of Brooke Bond tea before mucking about in his pool. We splash one another and chat about visiting Koech in the hospital. We jump off the diving board, float around on a plastic raft, then suntan on lounge chairs.

Kulvinder gabs on about his daddy.

"Mummy's always screaming at the daft prick 'cause he drinks too much booze," *he says.*

Cor. Alcohol. That's pretty bad. "Blimey!"

"'Blimey!' What kind of poncey word is that?" *He sips Lucozade through a straw.* "Anyway, whenever the daft prick drinks too much, he pulls me onto his lap." *He chews on his bottom lip.* "I hate it. His breath smells like crap, and it makes me sick." *He tinkles a bell and a houseboy, wearing white gloves, fetches our empty glasses.* "Want something to eat?" *Kulvinder asks.*

I nod.

"Ninataka papai," *Kulvinder says.*

"Ndiyo, bwana," *the houseboy replies.*

We return to our conversation. "Mummy doesn't do anything to stop Daddy. She's too busy nattering about adding rooms to the house at Mombassa."

The Sharmas own three homes; their third has a view of the long-billed flamingoes and pelicans of Lake Naivasha.

The houseboy returns with two slices of pawpaw, then stands beside us at attention.

Kulvinder waves him away. "Wende, wende."

Clutching a handbook of Ghandiji's finer aphorisms I set out
to confront the doddy bastard. I rehearse a high-handed
speech.

Have you lost your mind? Have you taken leave of your
senses? You think hitting a woman makes you a man? Well,
here I am. Give it your best shot. Go on. I thought so.
Chicken shit. No. I think she should stay with Sam for a bit.
Just till things settle. You're damn right it won't happen again.
Damn straight.

"I was getting changed and she started cursing and picking up
after me. I told her to stop. But she doesn't listen to anyone.
You know her. She just went on about how I was acting like a
child." Kulvinder carefully arranges a stack of *Time* magazines
on Erica's mahogany coffee table. "I tried taking the clothes
from her. But she shoved me and started screaming that I
never talked about my dad and that I'd wind up alone if I
didn't open up to anyone. That was when I lost it."

"Kulvinder, I don't give a damn what she said. You shouldn't
hit her."

"You have no idea. She's always buzzing around, fussing
over me, and I can't stand it."

I decide to be mature, put my personal feelings aside and go
with hogwash. "She cares about you, man."

"Well, I can't deal with her on that level right now."

"How long has this been going on?"

"She was real supportive when I split with Steph. Real cool.
But it didn't take long before she got all up in my business.
She insisted on it. And since she'd been so nice before, I felt
obligated to put up with it."

"Why don't you try telling her?"

"What!"

"Forget that. Just get it together. There's a trip to Tokyo at stake here."

"Listen, she wants to get hitched next year. Bet she didn't tell you that. It's stressing me out, and I hate it. I hate it, Leeds. You have no idea what it's like going out with the bitch. None whatsoever. 'Who didn't use a coaster today?' 'Could you fetch some mortadella and brie from the deli?' Brie! All I want is a goddamned slice of pizza. Is that too much to ask?" He fluffs up her velour cushions. "I've tried doing the right thing, but it's too hard. I can't fit myself into this fantasy she's having about who we are. Marriage! I can't take it anymore."

I rifle through the pages of Ghandiji's aphorisms and wait for him to finish rearranging the brass-framed photographs on Erica's polished mantelpiece.

In the morning Mum and Dad are more animated than usual at the kitchen table.

They've been acting awful chummy since Dad aborted his cockamamie sit-down strike. Lots of "hey honey" or "hold on a sec, dear" as they pepper one another with smooches.

"Oh, Ahab, I forgot to pick up the dry-cleaning yesterday," Mum says. "You'll need your black suit for our meeting with the bank."

"Don't worry about it, dear. I can do it on my way to fetch Kuldip."

"Sweetheart, why don't I come with you? We'll make an outing of it. We can all go for a hike on Mount Seymour after lunch."

"That would be lovely. Let's go to that cooperatively run place with the dairy-free desserts first. Kuldip would like that."

Something is afoot, although I'm hesitant to make inquiries.

"Hikes! Coops! You two aren't smoking ganja now are you?" I ask.

"Oh John," Mum says. "The last time we did that your dad got sick."

"She's kidding," Dad says, winking at her.

I skip school to spend the day in the library. I have to write a paper on Wilfrid Laurier.

Sadly, his life and times don't hold my attention long. Vivian's all up in my head.

She's switched to some of Kioko's loopy treatments for her knee. The highlight is to focus on celestial light and take long steams with eucalyptus oil. But progress has been slow.

So I've been treating her to the best of Leeds Kipligat. Trotting out cheeky comedic routines with lots of nasty ha-ha's to jolly her out of her dark moods.

Unfortunately, it hasn't gone well.

"I'm lookin for a job." It's always a job. "God knows I could use the paper. There's somethin I should get. Retail. No problem. I got me an interview the day after tomorrow. That's my thing. Interviews. Get me in the door and look out. Whirburrbapblap. Give 'em my spiel. Boom. Could you start yesterday, they say? Maaan, it's hot in here. Don't you find it hot? Guess not. Look who I'm talking to, Shaka-fuckin-Zulu. What was I saying? Yeah, retail. Sellin shoes on commission. That's what I'm talkin about. Can't you just see it? 'Hello, can I fuckin help you?'"

I don't think she's ever actually made it to an interview.

"Oh that. I had an AA meeting, and a friend got the cake. I couldn't just up and split. 'Hey, congrats on being sober for a year, but I got to get.'"

It's odd behaviour, and I suspect the worst. She's back on the junk. Snorting lighter fluid. Mainlining bleach.

I cheer myself up by remembering that I haven't wanted to cut in a month. It's no longer one of my go-to options. Nor, for that matter, have I thought much about Svetlana or Slim and Jugs. A solid series of workouts has left me relatively satisfied with myself.

The rest of the day passes uneventfully. Although, due to unforeseen developments, I find out I'll have to spend the weekend at work.

It's good news. Barney's Warehouse received a huge contract to ship furniture to a major distributor in Alberta.

Ms. Granger, MBA, is flushed at the collar from excitement and pressure. Most of her statements are now completed with "if I don't stay on top of it, nothing gets done."

She busts people's chops and only has one crying jag in her office.

It's all quite sexy.

I answer phones, send faxes, make appointments and write letters. All the while staving off her constant interruptions.

"John, can you copy this?" Or "Be a sweetheart and file these with the E-78's. If I don't stay on top of it, nothing gets done."

Despite the extended hours and increased responsibilities, I won't see any increased numbers on my paycheque. Instead Ms. Granger, MBA, plans a morale-boosting staff dinner midweek.

On Wednesday the Barney's Furniture Warehouse team meets at Mario's. Surprise: there's Coach, snogging with a twenty-something imp who has green tattoos on her arms.

"Marilyn is a painter," he tries to explain.

"That's Marilyyn. No last name, two y's. I used to be one of his athletes."

It's awkward. Nobody seems to know what else to say.

"How did you find working with Sam, Marilyyn?" I finally ask.

"Well, I'm glad to be doing something else, if that's what you mean." Sam flicks her hand off his arm. "He keeps trying to coax me back. But I'm done with the grind."

"Not me," I reply. "There are just too many meets I want to go to."

"That's right," Sam says. "And you'll get to them all."

Then Marilyyn gets dull. She talks about her latest art work before finishing with a story about a Greek play. The hero's mother devours her son during a wild sexual orgy.

I have no idea why she's telling me any of this.

"I better get back to my table," I say.

She hands me a card. "Come by sometime and see what I'm doing at the gallery. Marilyyn. No last name. Two y's."

"It's fine work," Sam adds.

Sam calls me later that night.

He denies anything is happening with Marilyyn. They're friends.

I don't say too much. I feel for Kiki.

I'm the only one to show up at Thursday's practice.

"Hey," Sam says.

"Hmmm." I'm not into him.

He lights up another smoke.

I slip on my spikes and sluggishly start in on the first of ten 600's.

"Pick it up, Leeds."

I coast down the backstretch.

Cut me a little slack, asshole. At least I made it to practice.

"33, 34, 35. Thirty-five seconds. That's too slow."

Fuck him. I can't be expected to put the hammer down every time out.

I maintain my form on the home stretch by keeping my strides long and my shoulders relaxed.

"68, 69, 70."

Good, only two hundred to go.

I lope into the final turn.

I should lift my knees more, but screw it. I just want to get the workout over with and get away from him.

"1.36. You're going to have to do much better than that."

I jog the 400-metre recovery out in lane six.

The adulterer ought to thank his lucky stars that I even showed up. Kulvinder and Erica had "an appointment," Vivian is a flake, and since I've been kicking ass of late, an easy day isn't going to hurt me.

I run the next three progressively slower, and by the time I'm done with the fifth one, Sam is nowhere in sight.

I find him sitting in his truck in the parking lot. The engine is running, and he clutches the steering wheel.

"People say that Keino beat Ryun in the 1500 at Mexico City because of the altitude. But they should have said, because of his attitude. Keino was hungrier on the day." He reaches for a lighter. "If you get that, I mean, if you really get what I'm saying here, you may have a shot at a scholarship.

But it won't happen if you continue pussy-footing around like you're doing." He sparks up. "Let me tell you something. Do with it what you will. Forget about me. Don't let your perception of *my* failures as a person be *your* excuse. My biggest disappointment is that I never became the athlete I wanted to be. You know why? I didn't show up hungry each and every day. I let my disappointment in others dictate how much effort I made." He stabs the cigarette out in an over-flowing ashtray. "It tears me up to see how much you kids take for granted. You have so much that we didn't have. We ran on asphalt. Did you know that? My first track spikes were nails hammered into the bottom of a pair of running shoes. We didn't have all the advantages that you have. But, as they say, youth is wasted on the young." He squeezes another smoke between his lips. "If you're going to have a legitimate shot at the Junior team, you'll have to be willing to lead a race from start to finish."

"Sod that." I should never have got suckered into believing in him. "I'm a kicker. I'm going to draft off the leaders for the first seven. Then bam. Smoke 'em like Wolhunter in Munich."

"That's the attitude I'm talking about. If the pace is slow at Nationals, you'll give less confident runners a shot at something you should have already claimed as your own. Filbert Bayi surprised Walker in Christchurch by getting out fast. Jipcho and Keino ambushed Ryun by doing the same in Mexico City."

"Hey, there's more than one way to skin a cat."

He crushes the unlit smoke into the ashtray. "This isn't going anywhere. Pack up your things. I'm taking you home. You've got some serious thinking to do before we meet again."

I get in and try not to fixate on his tobacco-stained fingers or his belly, which bumps against the steering wheel.

I remember his basement hallway, where those pictures of him hurdling were hung. Then I think of what he just said about attitude. He hadn't a clue then that the days he thought were failures would be the best it got for him.

Over dinner Mum and Dad reveal their big secret, but I'm not really paying attention. They're back in business, this time with Mrs. Sharma as a silent partner. They've rented a store on Commercial Drive and will specialize in selling goods from Africa: wooden carvings, *kiondos*, *kibuyus*, *kitenges* and drums.

"There's bound to be a steady flow of enthusiastic clientele," Mum says.

"These people love that world-beat music," Dad adds. "So our goods will make a wonderful complement to their safari through sound."

"Oh! Tell him about the . . ."

"Yes. We'll import from small markets in the Rift Valley and make certain the locals are suitably compensated. With the exchange rates as they are, we'll still manage to operate at a profit."

I want no part of it. The summer season is getting closer, and Sam's got Filbert Bayi on the brain.

I excuse myself, go to my bedroom and listen to Dad's audio tapes tell me how strong and powerful I am.

Sam calls me to go over the details of his plan.

My workouts will become more individualized as we shift from mileage to speed endurance. I'll continue to run six-milers in the morning and do weights three times a week. But the rest will change. Monday and Friday will be for long reps at race pace with a bunch of calisthenics thrown in between, and Wednesdays for quick pyramids—200, 300, 400, 500, 600, 800, 600, 500, 400, 300, 200, with a 200 jog between each. That'll leave Tuesday and Thursday for a second six-miler and Sunday for a ten-mile fartlek.

"'The people who get on in this world are the people who get up and look for the circumstances they want and, if they can't find them, make them.' I want you to think about that. No, scrap that. I'd prefer you act on it."

"Mistakes don't matter. It doesn't matter to me if you overextend yourself early in a race and have to suck it up at the end. All that is important is honest effort. 'In some attempts, it is glorious even to fail.'"

Why am I listening to the hypocrite? He's probably lying next to Marilyyn in a motel room.

Can't he get it through his thick skull? Leading isn't my strength. Sure, I admire the bloke, but I'm not Joaquim Cruz. I don't have forty-four-second 400-metre speed. I'll be better off running my own race. Conserve energy early before blowing everyone's socks off at the finish.

3

The following morning I'm on my way out to work when Erica calls.

"Did you see Kulvinder last night?"

"No. Why?"

"He said he wanted to surprise me yesterday afternoon, something big to make up for our fight. But he didn't come by the apartment, and his mother has no idea where he is."

"I don't follow."

"Did he say anything about his plans when you spoke last?"

"Christ, Erica. I said I didn't see him."

"Think about it. Anything unusual?"

I pull the receiver away from my ear. Count to five. Then, "Nah. Nothing."

"I'll never forgive him for this."

I'm fifteen minutes late, and Ms. Granger, MBA, is peeved.

"We've had this talk, John."

222

"I'm sorry," I murmur. Then find myself blubbering nonsensically about Kulvinder going AWOL and how I'm under all sorts of pressure because of track.

"Listen to me, Leeds. I realize you're juggling a lot of plates right now. But things aren't as overwhelming as they appear. You're only seventeen."

"Eighteen."

"Eighteen. So your life seems more difficult than it really is. Trust me. Take the Nationals as a for-instance. It's just one race."

"Well, I'm almost eighteen."

"Don't lose sight of your other options. I've watched you and think you've got what it takes to get a business degree."

"Thanks, Ms. Granger."

"As the N.A.A.C.P. says, a mind is a terrible thing to waste," she says.

"Indeed."

"Just stay an extra fifteen minutes at the end of your shift. Okay?"

"Okay."

So I found out what happened. Kulvinder emptied the cash register at the restaurant and partied with a hooker in a motel at an undisclosed location. They got tanked to the gills before a friend of hers joined them for a session of kinky-ass three-way.

Room service found him penniless, gagged and swishing about in a bathtub of his own urine.

However, the Erica-friendly version has it that Kulvinder needed to get away for a good think. One he returned from with a dozen long-stemmed roses, a bottle of Chablis, a compelling disclosure about his dad and a marriage proposal.

"Have you lost your friggin mind?"

"Give me a break."

"Goddamnit, Kulvinder. She doesn't even make you happy."

Wearily he looks at me. "Love has very little to do with happiness. Relationships are about making it through the long haul. The key is to develop the kind of companionship that will enable us to wipe one another's asses when we're old and decrepit."

"Perhaps you should leave the last part out of your marriage vows."

"You may not agree with my choices. But they are, after all, mine to make. I'm going to U.B.C. and running with Sam."

"Erica's really got your number."

"Don't you see? We're stable. Sam won't run us into the ground like they do over there. Canada has a pretty good carding system. If you're internationally ranked, you get a stipend."

"Listen to yourself."

"Hey, things between Erica and I aren't perfect. We have our moments, but that's the nature of the beast." He ought to be standing on a soapbox for this one. "You see, it really doesn't matter who you end up with. You're inevitably going to go through grief. You just have to decide whether that person is the one you're willing to go through all of that with." He folds a stick of gum into his mouth. "It's time for us to step up. We're not getting any younger you know."

"Kulvinder, that girl fantasizes about living in places with oak floors."

"Your point?"

"You're stealing from the restaurant."

"Not anymore."

"Right. Until the next time you decide to impress her by putting out for a sharkskin handbag."

"Cut the chicken-soup psychobabble," he replies. "Listen, I messed up. It won't happen again. Can we move on?"

I'm disappointed. I've spent far too much time being concerned about everyone else. Is Vivian destroying herself? Should Kulvinder break up with Erica? Why would Sam cheat on Kioko? Is he right about the kind of race I should run? Am I obligated to pitch in with the folks?

What's the use?

I stalk over to the store, sit the folks down and tell them I won't be involved with their latest business venture. That's their dream, not mine.

"We'll manage, Son," Mum says.

"A customer just came in, John," Dad says. "We'll talk about this later."

I ring up Sam and lay it on the line. I'm going to race with my own tactics this summer.

"You can lead a horse to water," he replies. "But you can't make it drink."

Whatever.

4

The next two weeks are a struggle, and I find myself going over every remotely painful incident I've ever experienced. Everything.

There was the day Dad yelled at me for breaking a teapot. The soccer game in which I had one man to beat and ended up losing the ball. The time I tripped on a rock and needed stitches in my wrist, on and on.

I lie in bed an extra half-hour in the morning. The blankets are pulled over my head, and I listen to the sound of smashing glass.

Making myself do the simplest of tasks is an ordeal. Getting dressed. Pouring myself a bowl of cereal. Holding a conversation with the folks.

I think about eating mangoes with Svetlana on a deserted isle.

It takes caffeine to get me out the door.

Workouts are chores to be ticked off a list. There's no spark. No interest, only a desire to crawl back into bed.

I even take sombre and reflective walks alone on the beach. Bending down to collect pebbles. Skipping stones off the surface of the sun-glazed ocean. Counting waves that lap on the shore.

Fortunately, everyone else is far too preoccupied with his or her own life to notice, and I'm too engulfed by misery to give a shit.

5

May.

"Do you need an umbrella?" Erica asks Sam as we stand in pissing rain at the start line. "You're getting soaked."

He dismisses her with a wave.

"At least put your hood up," Kulvinder adds. "We wouldn't want you to catch your death out here."

"Two sets of five 400's with a 400 jog recovery between each and a six-minute rest between sets," Sam says.

Rain. Perfect. The elements are stacked against me as well.

"He's ticked at you all," Viv teases. She's in an excellent mood. Her knee is better, and she's ready to run on the track again.

"Yeah, he's giving us the gears," Kulvinder says.

"On your mark."

"Come on, Sam," Erica says. "We've been a little distracted lately, but that's over." Kulvinder squeezes her arm.

"I'm not giving anyone 'the gears,' as you call it." His clothes stick to his skin. "I'm only trying to get this workout underway. Now is not the time to get complacent. We need to focus our attention on making an honest effort. Not for any reward that may or may not await us at the end of it all. But because we must be like Prometheus and choose life."

"You're such a drama queen," Vivian says.

We crack up, and even Sam smiles.

"Kulvinder, be a sweetie and get the umbrella out of my bag," Erica finally says.

He trots off, and we all collapse laughing.

I breathe deeply, lower my head and break the first 400 into one-hundred-metre segments.

Accelerate into the first curve, lean and allow momentum to carry you through.

My form feels choppy. But I adjust on the backstretch by keeping everything tall.

Hit your butt with your heel. Stretch forward with the ball of your other foot.

I wobble slightly off-centre and drift out of lane one into lane two but adjust by pointing my hips where I want my feet to go.

200 metres left. Don't think about the finish line. Just loosen the hands. Don't clench them. Hug the inside of the bend and don't cock your head.

When Kulvinder pulls up beside me on the home straight I relax and barrel forward. Concentrating on a spot five metres after the finish line.

"54, 55, 56, 57."

"Fifty-seven. Not bad."

I begin to jog.

"Finish it, Erica," Kulvinder shouts. "Right the way through. That's it." I slow down and wait for him to join me.

"How's it feel?" I ask.

"Piece of cake. I'll lead the next one. We can alternate."

The rain picks up and we end up splashing through puddles, our spikes heavy with water. But working together lightens the load.

By the time we round the final bend on the last 400, I'm still relatively fresh.

"Fifty-five seconds," says Sam.

We shout encouragement at the girls as they sprint up the straight. Erica finishes with a fifty-nine and Vivian strides in four seconds later. Then we all go on a warm-down jog.

It's been a good session.

While we stretch under the bleachers, Kulvinder suggests we catch a late movie at the repertory theatre.

"Let's flip for it," Erica says. "Heads for the South American and tails for the French."

"It's tails," Kulvinder says.

"Make it two out of three," Viv grumbles.

"Tails again."

"Don't sweat it, Viv," Erica says. "European films usually have lots of male frontal nudity."

"Dick action. I could go for some of that."

Kulvinder and I buy goodies while Erica and Vivian find us seats.

"I hope the movie isn't another arty drag," I say. "Heavy symbolism is lost on me."

"You're fucked. It's loosely based on the life of Pablo Picasso."

"Any sex scenes?"

"S'pose so, but tastefully done. Soft lighting, moody use of camera angles, the works."

The line limps forward. "Hey, bet you didn't know Pablo Picasso was African?"

"Bollocks."

"I'm serious. His real name was Kwame Igbwenuke. He was the son of a Nigerian fisherman and an Italian dressmaker. He had to change his name to Picasso in order to make it in the art salons. Look it up. People went batty over him after that. Gertrude Stein wanted him to do her portrait. Ernest Hemingway . . ."

He punches me in the arm. "You should write an essay."

"I would," I reply. "But I think my ideas are still a little ahead of their time."

I scrunch down beside Vivian and divvy out the food. Then the house lights dim, and the trailers begin.

The first one is about a soldier's disheartening return from war. The wife's buggered off with the milkman, and the old neighbourhood is now controlled by a sorry collection of unruly thugs. The second trailer tells the tale of a mad film-maker with the hots for his nymphet lead. Plenty of gang bangs and broody musing about the meaning of art.

Vivian interrupts. "Aren't you going to hold my hand?"

"Oh, I didn't think . . ." She pushes the box of popcorn aside and reaches for my sweaty mitt.

The feature gets underway, and we're treated to the work of a director in decline. The sumptuous pans over tablecloths, curtains and easels take months. The segues into dream sequences are overdone; there are far too many long robes, masks and filthy allusions to Freud. The characters . . . well, by the end of the first hour, it doesn't matter. Vivian has her hand on my cock.

When I get home that night, I find Dad reading a book in the kitchen.

"You're home, Son."

"Yeh."

I'm in a great mood and relax into the seat beside him. "What are you reading?"

He holds up the cover. "It's John Stuart Mills . . ." Abruptly he grabs my wrists. Shit. I forgot to roll down the sleeves of my sweater after messing around with Viv. "My God." Dad stares at wounds that have healed into small bumpy scars.

"Let go."

He tears up. "What have I done?"

"Let go."

The room blurs. I'm nauseous. If I don't bolt to the toilet, I'll double over with dry heaves.

"I had to put the family first, Son."

"You put yourself first," I yell. "Nobody asked you to get involved in redeveloping the slum!"

I grind my teeth and plunk down on the sofa. I can't keep my hands from tapping my thigh.

"I'm your father," he mumbles. "Don't you get that? I did what had to be done." I notice flecks of gray at his temples. "I did what had to be done."

"We never should have left."

"I know it hurts, Son."

"Stop." I feel like a clumsy little boy.

"I understand."

He plops down next to me and wraps an arm around my shoulders.

"No." I try to pull away. "No."

He grips tight. "I understand." Holding onto me while the pain dislodges from its mooring.

When I wake up, it's dark, and voices mutter in the driveway.

Mr. Sharma talks to Dad. "They're coming for you tonight."

"This can't be happening," Dad replies.

"What are you going to do?"

"There must be a mistake."

"Ahab, this is happening."

I hyperventilate and crawl under my bed.

The front door bangs open, and footsteps echo through the house.

I hold my breath, but my heart won't stop hammering.

Feet clip-clop into my room; someone snatches back the blankets, and I can't hold my breath much longer.

I exhale loudly.

The outline of a head appears, and I crawl back against the wall.

"Shh." It's Mum. "We have to leave. Now."

"Did you find Koech?"

"Not yet."

"What if he comes back and we're not here?" I ask.

"Shh. No questions, Son," she replies. "We have to leave right away."

Outside Dad shakes Mr. Sharma's hand. "Thank you," he says.

"You'd do the same for my family, I'm sure."

"What's going on?" I ask.

"Emmanuel has arranged for us to lay low at their cottage in Mombassa," Dad whispers.

"You'll be safe there, John," Mr. Sharma adds.

"Wait." I run back inside to fetch Koech's track top and army boots. By the time I return to the driveway, Kulvinder and Mrs. Sharma have joined the fray.

We climb into separate cars and, with the headlights turned off, drive away from home.

Dad and I sag against each other, my shoulder wedged into his armpit. We are besieged by the rheumy kitchen light.

6

At the following workout I run a 1000-metre time trial in 2.24.37. Sam says that translates to about 1.53 for the eight. It's my best ever at a distance I seldom run.

I've never been fitter.

When I'm around the folks, they treat me with kid gloves. They ask about my day and make sure nothing controversial comes up in our conversations. It's as if they're afraid that the wrong word will have me carving up my wrists.

My spare time is spent with Vivian. We're "hanging out," not as a couple, but like friends who think nothing of going down on each other. "Will's history," she says. "We're both different than we was at thirteen. But don't go getting no ideas. I ain't ready to jump into a situation, kn'a mean?"

It's cool with me. We don't have to worry about one person putting in more effort than the other. None of that. We just mess around when the mood strikes. Which, thankfully, is a lot.

On Saturday night the Achilles track athletes go to a party. The season begins in a week, and we need a major distraction before the big push.

Vivian and Erica spend the night on a crowded dance floor in a revamped artists' studio. They press their hips together, simulate going down on one another and run fingers through one another's hair.

Kulvinder and I do shots of gin on the couch.

Bodies swim like fish around the muggy fourteenth-floor apartment. They splash past tables and chairs to lurk in corners of the cramped room. Some linger for a time in the kitchen. Others flop on the furniture, and the rest move in schools across the dance floor.

I squeeze off the top of a beer. "To our women," I toast.

"Touché," Kulvinder says.

We breathe in the smoky air.

"You seem calmer," I say.

"I think I'm closer to where I'd like to be." He slides a slice of salted lemon between his lips then downs a shot. "Erica's had a lot to do with that."

"Then it's all good," I reply.

"Most definitely." He suppresses a belch. "It looks as if you've got something solid going on there with Vivian."

"I think we might."

"You over Svetlana?"

"Most of the time."

"That's what I like to hear, mate. You couldn't be doing much better. Viv's a real looker."

"Whoa. Slow down there, cowboy."

When Kulvinder lifts the next shot to his mouth, gin spills onto his fingers. He laughs.

"What's so funny?" I ask.

"Me," he says. "Daddy used to spill his drinks like this all the time. The fruit doesn't fall far from the tree, you know."

I swish foam around at the bottom of my beer glass.

He salts another lemon and downs another shot, then blows Erica a kiss.

By two o'clock in the morning the two of us haven't budged an inch. Meanwhile Erica and Vivian have drifted into the kitchen, where they join a small group breaking plates against the floor.

"I think it's time to leave," Kulvinder slurs.

"I don't think I can move."

"Well, if you manage to get your butt up off that chair, I'll drive you to Mummy's. She's away on business again, so we'll have the run of the place."

Mrs. Sharma lives in Burnaby now, and we huddle together on the veranda of the house, fighting to stay awake.

Vivian straddles me. "Let's get jiggy till dawn."

"I'm tired," Erica mumbles. Her head is lodged in Kulvinder's lap.

"Yo, don't be such pussies," Vivian says. "We still be where the party at. So get up on . . ." I don't hear the rest because I nod off.

I'm woken by the sound of scraping on the roof.

I walk onto the lawn and look up. Vivian is perched on a ledge with a bottle of liquid detergent in her hand.

"What the hell?"

"I can see downtown from here," she shouts.

"Shhh, you're going to wake up the neighbours."

"I'll do whatever the fuck," she yells. "Whatever the fuck."

Kulvinder and Erica run outside.

"That shit she's drinking is poisonous," Erica says.

"I'll get a ladder," Kulvinder offers.

"Do y'know I love y'all more than Ali meant to Frazier?" Vivian replies.

"We love you too," Erica says.

"More than cola's a part of coke?"

"Please, Vivian." A light goes on in a room across the street. "Just get down from there," I urge.

"Do y'all love me?"

"Yes," we reply. "Yes."

Kulvinder returns with a ladder. "I've got a firm grip on it," he says. "Just move towards it."

She starts to chant. "One, two, three, four. Who the fuck we rootin for? Vivian. Vivian." She tries kicking up a leg, but her knees buckle and moss drops to the ground. "Ooops."

"Goddamnit, Viv." I say. "Stop mucking about."

She regroups. "Righteo, ladies and germs. Righteo." She gives shuffling forward a stab, but totters off-balance.

"Keep your eyes on the ledge," I plead.

Vivian inches towards the ladder.

Once she's on the ground, we force her to drink two cartons of milk, and she pukes into the can.

"Shouldn't she get her stomach pumped?" Erica asks.

I check the bottle of detergent. "She didn't drink very much."

"Thank heavens," Erica replies.

I wait out the vomiting, wipe Vivian's mouth with a flannel and tuck her into Mrs. Sharma's double bed.

"Know what?" she mumbles.

"Get some rest."

"My mom's real sick." Her eyelids flicker as she falls asleep.

Kulvinder and Erica gather their gear for a three o'clock
workout. They gather around Vivian, who's propped up in the
bed on satin pillowcases.

"We'll smooth things out with Sam." Kulvinder embraces
her. "Mummy doesn't get back till Tuesday, so stay as long as
you need to."

"Thanks."

Erica kisses Vivian's cheeks and rubs her belly. "If there's
anything I can do?" She extends her pinkie and thumb into a
makeshift phone and holds it up to her ear. "Call me."

When they leave, I scrunch in beside her. "Can I get you
anything?" I ask.

"That was some fuckin weekend."

"Are you sure? Mrs. Sharma keeps her fridge stocked with
healthy food."

"Don't look at me like that," she says.

"Like what?"

"Like I'm a piece of shit."

"I'm not."

"I done horrible things."

"We all have."

"Bet nobody cut out on they moms 'cause she had lung
cancer."

She clams up, flicks on the television and surfs.

I don't press.

7

The first race of the season is in Eugene, Oregon. Kulvinder, Erica and Sam are laid up with the flu, so it's just Vivian and I.

We both fuck up.

Vivian tries her hand at the eight, runs out in lane three for the first 500 to avoid getting spiked, but when she moves up on the back stretch, she gets boxed in and trips on another runner's heels. She has to be helped to the medic's tent.

I expect to run well because my build-up going in is solid. But I still put in a pathetic effort and finish a discouraging seventh in 2.01.33.

My bad. I'd thrown in a session of 200's in twenty-two seconds the day before, despite Sam's insistence on taking it easy. They were supposed to help get the travel rust out of my legs. But the plan backfired, and I was overtired.

It's foggy as we drive back to Vancouver in a rental, and we can't get anything on the car radio.

"We should have stayed overnight," I mumble.

"I only suggested we bounce," Vivian snaps. "You didn't have to agree."

"You don't suggest. You demand."

She fingers her temples. "Step off, black. You're giving me a fuckin headache."

A truck whips by in the lane beside us and splashes rainwater onto the windshield.

I slow down to fifty.

"Pull over."

"There you go again. Do this. Don't do that. I'll pull over when I want to."

The car begins to skid. First hitting an embankment on the passenger side. Then sliding across the lane, banging up against a guardrail and spinning to a standstill facing oncoming traffic.

I turn the key in the ignition. But the engine won't turn over. Try again.

My fingers are a pair of fucking stumps.

Vivian panics. "I'm outta here."

A car glances off my door and disappears into the fog. Another tags the bumper, pushing us forward.

"Yo, fuck that," she says.

I can hear a semi approaching. Breathe in. Relax. Then turn the key again.

Nothing.

"My door's jammed," Viv shrieks.

I close my eyes, turn the key and pump the accelerator. The engine sputters then stammers and fires up. I pull off to the side of the road, and the truck rumbles past.

We're fortunate. The car's banged up—the front hood is mulch. But neither one of us is hurt.

The engine rattles while we drive towards the nearest town.

By the time we get to the closest gas station, the mechanic has turned in for the evening. So we leave the car and foot it in search of a motel.

"We're full," says a shrunken, bent man sitting behind a counter next to a black Bible.

We pass a vacancy sign on our way to the sidewalk. "Bloody liar," I say. "We should make him put us up."

"I ain't mixing it up with no crackers tonight," she replies. "I'm tired."

The next rest spot is half a mile down the road. I flash a roll of twenties, and we're given keys to a room.

"I got to take a leak," I say.

"G'wan then."

I tremble so much that I pee all over the floor. Unsteadily I make my way back to the bedroom.

"You're shaking, yo," Vivian says.

"I don't feel so good."

She touches my hands. "They're fuckin freezing, too." She warms them up against her cheeks.

I'm skittish as I pick my way towards the elastic band of her panties, find the outline of her pubic hair and scout a soft trail between her hips.

Her tiny hand explores my skin. Pauses at my hipbone.

Her eyes are shut; wind rushes against the window.

What is she thinking?

I push forward, placing myself between her legs.

Bed springs squeak, and her nipples brush my chest, slathered with sweat.

She reaches for my hips, pulling me towards her. Fast. Hard.

Until I lose my bearings and hurl myself at her, flesh smacking against bone.

A screen door bangs open, and I can hear the wind blow debris through the motel's parking lot.

"I love you," I say. Pretty certain that I mean it.

When we get back to Vancouver, Vivian acts all aloof.

She doesn't return my calls and makes excuses about why we can't get together. There are appointments to see a physio. Job interviews to go to. The works.

I know both her mum's cancer and her injury have hit her hard. But it's no excuse.

By the time I toe the line at a high performance meet in Burnaby, I'm in a dark mood. Keen to make amends for having let myself get lured into voicing my feelings for her.

I don't give a rat's ass who's in the field: get out fast and lead when we break the stagger.

Some bloke stays with me through the first 350. But I'm not having it. Not today.

I ratchet it up a notch.

"51, 52, 53."

I split in fifty-two seconds. Suicidal maybe. But it feels easy.

I look over my shoulder at 500. I'm ten metres up on the field, and there's still plenty of jump in my legs.

Everything's happening the way I want. I think, accelerate, and I do. I say, relax, and my body responds. I'm inside the moment, no longer scrambling to get ahead of it.

A cool breeze tickles my eyes. Froth sits on my upper lip, and I free-fall forward into overdrive.

I run 1.51.08.

Breaking two minutes was a barrier I hadn't been entirely certain I'd ever get over. But I'd smashed the hell out of the bugger and run eight seconds better than Kulvinder's best. Not just that. I did it alone, with no one to pace me. Just me out there pushing the pace like Koech used to.

Best of all, it's late May, and I know I can only get faster.

I celebrate by going for an easy jog in a park beside the stadium.

The sky seems bluer than usual, and I can hear the wind rustling among the leaves.

8

Kulvinder bounces back from his sickness to clock an eight in 1.51.19 the following weekend. It's eleven-tenths slower than my p.b.

He's pleased with his breakthrough, and, after a spirited fifteen-second debate, coughs up enough money to get us a lap dance at a strip joint.

"Erica will be intrigued by how you spend playtime with your boy."

"Not if he keeps his trap shut."

We sit at the bar and order a couple of cran-and-vodkas.

"All you have to do is pick out a stripper that you fancy," Kulvinder says.

"Enough already," I reply. "You told me that over twenty times."

"Right then." He points to a tall blonde with a shiny rhinestone bikini. "You're on your own."

I take in the final set on the main stage, where the dancer tips her breast implants towards the drunken mutts in the front row.

"You gonna sit here all night?" It's a hefty biker chick wearing nasty leather underthings. "Or do you wanna party?"

I follow her into a room in the back and get set up in a cushy armchair right next to Kulvinder.

"What's your name?" she asks.

"Leeds."

"Leeds, you get three songs at forty hits a pop," she says. "No talking and don't even think about touching."

I nod while she drops her drawers.

Kulvinder groans beside me. "Holy fuck. Yeh. Fuck, yeh."

Listening to him is dampening my groove.

Before I can signal him to pipe down, biker chick straddles me and rides me like a Harley. "Vroom," she says. "Vrooooom."

I cut her loose after two songs. I can't take the sound of Kulvinder crying for bloody mercy.

I figure I'll wait it out at the bar and on his return talk him into leaving early.

After three more drinks he still hasn't reappeared.

Jesus, I hope he didn't grope and get tossed out on his ear.

On my way over to check up on him, I'm approached by a petite brunette.

"Help." She looks over my shoulder. "There's someone following me." I turn around. "Don't look!"

"Should I get a bouncer?"

"No," she says. "It's one of the bouncers."

"I'll get you out of here if you want."

"No. Act natural." She grabs my hand and leads me to the private room.

Kulvinder's still where I left him, the biker chick riding him.

Petite brunette pushes me onto the empty chair as a hopped-up bouncer enters the doorway. My body stiffens, and she gets busy shaking her rack into my face. "He's my boyfriend," she whispers. "We had a fight this morning, and he damn near broke my arm."

"Vrooooom," I hear beside me. "Vrooooom."

By the time I manage another look at the door, he's gone.

"He doesn't think I'm doing enough to earn." She strips down. Above her shaven pussy is a tattoo of a lantern.

"Are you sure you don't want to leave?" I ask.

"Certain."

Nervously I chuckle. Stuck at the way her lips brush close to mine and the way she places my hand on her nipple.

Six hundred bucks later, Kulvinder and I stumble, wasted, onto the street.

"What a bizarre night." I wave at a cab.

"Bet it took your mind off Vivian, though."

"You got that right." The taxi slows on its approach. The cabbie takes a good look at us, then picks up speed and whizzes past.

"Could you talk to her for me?" I wave at another. "Just to find out what's up."

"I'm there, mate," he says. "I'm there."

Two days later Vivian stops by in the afternoon. Coming on all breathless and harried while we sit in the kitchen drinking grape juice.

"Kulvinder hit on me," she says.

I grit my teeth and gulp. Heat builds in my jawbone.

"Don't you have a motherfuckin reaction?"

I look away. "Did you sleep with him?"

"Of course not," she replies. "You must think I'm some kinda ho?"

"No. I'm talking crap. Sorry."

"Yo, why you sweatin me? I didn't do nothin wrong."

"Right. It wasn't you that's been avoiding me the last two weeks."

"Don't get white on my ass with that sarcasm shit." She reaches out for my hand. "I didn't fuck Kulvinder."

I pull away. "And I'm supposed to be grateful?"

She gathers herself with a couple of deep breaths. "I screwed up, a'ight?" She grabs hold of my hand again and holds it tight. "But how was I gonna tell you the truth? I've been bugged out since I got injured. I chucked my lithium, and I been snortin just about anything I could cop."

The corners of her eyes twitch.

What else is she lying about? Her mum. Screwing Kulvinder. What? "Things have gotten too crazy out-of-control. I don't know where I'm headed no more."

She picks up her glass, but it drops to the floor.

"Dumb cunt," she mumbles, scrambling to clean up. "Stupid clit. I can't even . . . what a dumb cunt." I stoop down beside her.

She's clutching shards of broken glass.

Slowly I open her hand.

There's blood on her palm, and I pick glass out of her cuts.

We go see Sam together, and by the end of the day she's checked into detox and back on a heavy dose of lithium.

I see Kulvinder at practice, and the bugger makes a show of how happy he is to see me. "My man," he says. "How goes tricks?"

"Never better," I reply.

I go over my options while we warm up. I could bust his chops. I could hip Erica to our night on the town. I could end our friendship and never talk to him again.

By the time we line up for a session of threes, I'm still undecided.

"These are supposed to be between thirty-four and thirty-five seconds," Sam announces. "I'd like you to be ready to go again by the time you've jogged the 300-metre recovery." He holds up his stopwatch. "Ready. Go."

In the middle of the first bend I whack Kulvinder in the bicep with an elbow. He pops me right back with a stiff forearm. I push him, and we trip together into the infield, rolling on the grass and beating one another with our fists. I get on top, drop a right cross into his cheek and stick a left hook in his jaw. He catches me with an upper cut, and I bite my tongue.

Erica and Sam separate us.

"What's all the fuss about?" Sam shouts.

Neither one of us responds.

"This type of competitiveness is over the line." I stare at Kulvinder, hatred seeping out of every pore. "From now on I don't want either of you to work out or race together. You can resolve whatever this is about on the track in Montreal." He retreats trackside to keep an eye on Erica.

"Stay away from Vivian, *dog*," I sneer.

"You stay away from me," he replies.

We lay low at the Sharmas' cottage on Diane Beach. Kulvinder and I are stuck together in a humid room with a view of the Indian Ocean.

We climb coconut trees, bury our feet in the white sand, collect small shells and chase crabs.

In the morning the two of us spend low tide collecting red starfish from the coral reef and prodding black sea urchins with sticks. There are schools of blue fish in puddles of clear water, where large brown crabs are curled up in holes.

"If Koech's knee mends quick, he'll still be able to have a go at breaking four minutes next year," I say.

"Easy, yeh." The tide's getting high, and we're on the reef far from the beach. "He's bound to turn up soon." Kulvinder pulls a crumpled pack of cigarettes from a pocket. "Want one?"

"Sure," I reply.

He strikes a match and lights up a couple.

"To Koech," he says shoving one between my lips.

"To Koech."

I gag.

"Don't blow it out your mouth. Swallow . . . like this."

He demonstrates, smoke entering his mouth and escaping from his nostrils.

I try again and choke, my eyes watering.

By the time I get it right, I'm dizzy, nauseous, and my chest hurts.

"Lads." It's Mr. Sharma, ambling along the reef towards us.

"Damn," Kulvinder says. "Do you think he saw us?"

We drop the cigs.

"I don't know."

We wait for him. "A word." He's ten feet away, and I worry about the smell on my breath. "I know what it's like to be young . . ." He slips, and his foot disappears into a hole up to the knee. "Shit." He tries to pull it out. "I'm stuck."

Kulvinder and I rush over and each grab an arm. Grunt. But he doesn't budge. I get a hold of his leg. Pull. Nothing.

"These damn football boots," Mr. Sharma says. "They're jammed under something."

The tide is coming in fast, and we have to get him out quick. I panic. "We need to get help."

We try to free his leg again, salt water enveloping our ankles. "Don't worry, Daddy," Kulvinder pleads. "We've got it."

We dig at the coral around his calf. But progress is slowed by a wave that leaves us on our knees.

"You lads are going to have to go," Mr. Sharma says. "No, Daddy."

"Go." He pulls a bottle of whisky from his pocket. "Go." "Daddy."

"Bugger off."

I grab Kulvinder's arm and we make a run for the beach. By the time we look back, Mr. Sharma's nowhere to be seen.

The rest is bits and pieces: boats searching the water for Mr. Sharma's body, fog horns, Mrs. Sharma wailing. "He'd been drinking, I never should have let him search the reef for the boys." My arm is flung around Kulvinder's shoulder, and we sit on a log at the beach. "This wouldn't have happened if we didn't come with you to this blasted place," he moans. I stare ahead at the brawling waves scrolling ashore. Turning into bubbles. Bursting.

9

June.

I get a call from Sam's contact at Villanova.

"Sam tells me good things about you," Mr. Farmer says. "He thinks you'll thrive in our track program up here."

"Wow."

"All of our 800-metre runners on scholarship have broken 1.50. That means you'll have to do the same if you plan to come here."

"No sweat."

"I must be frank, though. Our track budget has taken some hits in the past year, so the best we can do is offer you partial funding. But remember, that's contingent on whether you break 1.50 this season."

"Sounds great."

"We'll cover the cost of tuition and get you a job on campus to cover some of your living expenses. However, the difference will be up to you. That means coming up with approximately 5000 dollars."

"No problem."

"How are your marks?"

"B's."

"Good. Have you got your application forms in?"

"Uhuh."

"Excellent. You should hear soon. Good luck."

Unbelievable. Villanova's interested. All I have to do is run 1.49.0 and come up with five grand, US!

The folks are thrilled about the call.

"We're proud of you, Son," Dad says.

"Really?"

"Of course we are," Mum adds.

I'm surprised to find myself feeling chuffed that they've taken an interest. So I don't tell them about the cost. It'd only put a damper on things.

Their hard work is reaping benefits at the store; the capitalist venture moves forward in fits and starts. Some weeks are slow. People nip in, have a quick look around, try on the odd tie-dyed shirt and leave without a purchase. On other days Mum and Dad return home after banking enough to make them feel like successful entrepreneurs.

"Life is looking up," Dad says. "At the rate things are going, we'll be able to pay Kuldip back in a year and start saving for a place of our own." He flips to a dog-eared page in *The Economist*. "Those who accurately predict changes in the market are the ones who get ahead. Real estate is heading into a downturn. Nobody is buying. So we'll be sure to find us a bargain in the days to come."

"We mustn't get ahead of ourselves, dear."

"It doesn't hurt to plan ahead, honey," he says. "It's the only way the seemingly impossible becomes possible. Right, Son?"

In five days Vivian is back at Sam and Kioko's. She's irritable as shit and bored. But at least she's clean.

The next step is rehab: lots of telly over at Sam's, sitting through countless AA meetings together or taking in the odd flick.

Her season is over, and her priority is to follow through with the steps—admitting her powerlessness over alcohol and drugs, contacting a higher power, making a moral inventory of herself, and so on.

Relating to all this is like deciding to make an assault on the 800-metre world record without having the adequate fitness. I start acting like a spastic jackass because I'm afraid that if I let her out of my sight, something bad will happen. I arrange my schedule so we're together as much as possible, and ring her up during those rare moments when we're apart.

"Hey, Viv," I say. "Just wanted to see what you were up to."

"Same as a fuckin hour ago."

"Oh, I'm sorry. I shouldn't have called."

"No, it's cool." She sounds vexed.

"Weeeeell, I don't have anything to say."

"Me neither." She laughs. "See ya tomorrow."

When I get off the phone I beat myself up for interrupting her when she's most likely been working on step number four.

My workouts are going well; six twos in twenty-two point, four fours in fifty-one, and then back-to-back sixes in 1.20. But I can't seem to get it up on race days.

I run a couple of 400's in the mid forty-eights and three eights in the low 1.50's.

The eights are discouraging. I thought running faster would be a cinch. But it hasn't worked out that way. I can't seem to get my head into what I need to do.

I've been accepted at Villanova. But it's conditional. They want documents proving I'll be able to cover all my costs.

"There's no way in hell I'll be able to raise that kind of money," I complain to Vivian.

"So don't go," she replies.

"That's fucked." I hate that I can't have what I deserve. "There's always some cost that's either out of my price range or beyond my control."

"It ain't the end of the world," she says.

"It certainly feels like it."

"You still got options, yo," Viv says. "What about a student loan?"

"I guess."

"Hell, you're fit enough to shatter 1.50."

I sigh.

"Just handle your business," she continues. "Dig?"

"Yeh," I grumble. "I dig."

I try everything. Cold showers to get the blood pumping before warm-up. Reclining in bed all day before heading to the track. No nookie-nookie. Caffeine pills. I even mix things up tactically, getting out fast over the first four or laying back and pushing from the bell. But nothing helps. I don't run any better than 1.51.32, two-tenths slower than my personal best.

I talk to Sam.

"Any champion worth their weight in gold is bound to arrive at the crossroads," he says. "I see it all the time. It happened to me when I was twenty-one. I began to coach myself. Edwin Moses had done it successfully. I was going to do it too. It was a mistake, of course. I picked up nasty habits. Got lazy with my trail leg. Overtrained. And I almost didn't make the Commonwealth Games team in 'seventy-eight. The following year I set a national record. Don't misunderstand me. I'm not suggesting that you're bound to fail. Only that each pilgrim has their own particular lessons to learn on the road to Mecca."

My second-last chance to break through is at a meet in Eugene five days before Nationals.

I split in fifty-six and come back in fifty-four to clock 1.50.13. A p.b. by nine-tenths.

Kulvinder wins the 1500 in a respectable 3.44.58. The bastard. While Erica puts the finishing touches to a solid build-up with a best of 2.00.61 despite coasting over the final ten metres.

My body is moving fluidly again. Mecca is in sight, and Sam is pleased.

10

When we return to Vancouver, the oddest thing happens. I get up in the middle of the night to take a leak and almost black out. The sensation passes in a flash. But I can't shake the feeling of spaciness that accompanied it.

By morning I've got a fucker of a sore throat.

Vivian stops by, makes me plonk down an overdose of vitamin C, squeezes echinacea into a pot of ginger tea and tucks me into bed.

"You got four days to get it together," she says. "Suck it up."

I'm feverish. My body aches every time I move, and I drift in and out of sleep.

Since the folks are at work, Vivian stays with me. Whenever I open my eyes, I find her adjusting the curtains, force-feeding me soup, and wiping sweat from my forehead with a flannel.

"You don't have to do this," I mumble.

"It ain't no problem, yo," she says. "Just think of me as Florence fuckin Nightingale."

I drift off again. Only to awaken to find her ready to serve up a foul-smelling potion of ox bile and bat feet.

At noon the following day I'm shocked to find her sitting on the end of the bed. She slipped out at night but returned in the morning armed with tarot cards and a copy of the I-Ching.

I can't keep any food down and I have a chronic headache. But I'm grateful for her company.

At night she does a bang-up job of feeding the folks tall tales of my physical robustness: long walks we've taken, heavy meals I've eaten, healthy bowel movements I've been having. Precautionary measures to stave off any talk of not going to Montreal.

I take to watching the way white oblong patches from the sun imprint the side of her face or listening to the way she sometimes struggles for words.

It must be the capsules filled with ground-up tree bark she has me on.

The day before I'm supposed to leave, Vivian pushes me out the front door and loads a picnic basket into the back of Sam's truck.

"I'll drive," she says.

I scratch an itch at the brim of my cap.

She pulls me inside, turns out of the driveway, heads onto the main drag and turns off onto a side road.

After twenty minutes we stop beside a stretch of sand. She leads the way to the top of a dune before unpacking the picnic basket onto a blanket.

The occasional patch of long grass breaks up the landscape around us.

I scratch under the brim of my cap again.

"It's nice and deserted." She hands me a glass of spirulina juice.

I'm moved.

After downing our drinks, she clambers onto my chest and starts to tickle my underarms.

I writhe in agony. "Stop."

"You're ticklish."

"Stop."

She laughs. "A'ight."

"Don't ever fucking do that again."

"Whoa. Chill."

Thoughts of Koech start to bop around in my mind like popping corn, hot and random and confused.

I start to cry.

"What?" she asks.

"Nothing."

"Fess up, Leeds."

"Kulvinder screwed it all up."

"Slow down, boo. You losin me."

Kulvinder disappears into his house. On his return he's carrying a rifle.

"*Cripes, Kulvinder!*"

"*It's only Daddy's BB gun.*"

"*We're not going into the slum with that thing.*"

"*Are you getting all cry-baby on me again?*"

I don't reply.

We climb over spikes on the top of the front gate and drop down into a dusty lane. It's full of potholes, and our feet stir up puffs of red dust.

"That's where the French Ambassador lives." Kulvinder points to a brick house covered in trails of dark green ivy. "Did you know they can kill people and not go to jail?"

"Cor."

We creep forward, keeping Koech in sight. When we pass a high black gate bordered by two stone columns, a German shepherd, dripping saliva, snarls at us.

"Let's go back," I say.

"Don't be chicken," he responds.

The next couple of homes have huge sloping lawns on which shamba boys, shiny with sweat, trim hedges and water flower beds filled with bougainvilleas.

"You see that place?" Kulvinder nods towards a black marble veranda. "The son goes to boarding school at Eton in England. That's where I'm going when I'm twelve."

"Me too," I lie.

We stay out of sight, trailing after Koech until eventually he slides through a barbed-wire fence in front of an empty lot. His trousers catch as he pulls himself up and over a fallen tree then scrambles down a steep embankment.

Kulvinder and I crouch behind the tree then sneak a peak.

"It stinks," Kulvinder whispers.

"We should probably head back," I whisper, butterflies in my belly.

"Good idea."

I stand up, stumble on my ankle and fall against the tree. It gives way under my weight; I roll down the embankment and land, with a loud crack, in the side of a cardboard shack. It collapses, and I stare up into the face of a bony woman nursing a child.

"Oooweee," she shrieks. "Ooowee."

I scramble backwards and topple into sewage, a crowd of skeletal figures gathering around me.

I curl up into a ball, flies descending on my ears. My breath is forced. Then long thin fingers tighten around my shoulder.

"Let him go, fucking darkies," I hear Kulvinder shout. "Let him go." BAM BAM BAM.

People scamper in all directions to avoid BB-gun pellets. The woman cringes, shrieking and clutching her baby.

"Koech tried to make it right."

"We all do shit we're 'shamed of."

"You don't get it," I stammer. "He tried to set it straight."

"It ain't nobody's fault."

"And he isn't coming back."

"I know."

I hate that I'm crying and bawl even more, my head in her lap, her fingers wiping my sopping cheek.

The next day Vivian presses a packed suitcase into my hands, helps me to dress and sees me off at the airport.

"I'm gonna go hang with my Moms for a couple days," she says.

"You sure?"

"Yup."

"Right."

"Don't fuck up," she says, squeezing a necklace with a silver crucifix into the palm of my hand.

"You either," I reply, kissing her.

11

Sam, Kulvinder, Erica and I get into Montreal at around six in the evening.

My head is clearer, and I can digest light food. But the cold has travelled into my chest, and I'm coughing up phlegm.

Kulvinder and I haven't talked since the day we fought. There's so much forgetting that's gone into making us that I don't know where to start.

We're staying at the Holiday Inn. I share a fourth-floor room with Sam while Erica and Kulvinder shack up across the hall.

Sam unpacks super-size underpants into a drawer. "Once the heats get underway tomorrow, you won't even remember you're sick," he says, then buggers off to talk shop with some coaches.

I'm left alone, with way too much time to think about how difficult making the final will be.

William Bones, a student on scholarship at Rice, is one of several runners to watch. He was a finalist at the N.C.A.A.'s and broke 1.47 for the first time.

He's been running his races all season by hanging off the early pace and finishing strong.

Terrence Long, the gold-medallist last year, is the favourite. He clocked some quick times outdoors. His best of 1.47.12, run in Toronto earlier that summer, is no indication of how fast he's capable of going.

Long is also a kicker. So Sam figures they'll both lay back before pouncing hard off the final bend.

On paper Kulvinder and I are the next fastest. But Phil Lawlor, the silver-medallist last year, is also a threat.

The next day there's an enthusiastic crowd at Claude Robillard Stadium.

It's hot, and I warm up in the shade behind the stadium.

The top three plus the next two fastest qualify for the final. But I've caught a break. Phil Lawlor is the only seeded athlete in my heat.

What a relief. I still don't have any jump in my legs.

Both Erica and Kulvinder make it through to the final in convincing fashion. They control the pace of their heats and lead from start to finish.

I don't take any chances and lay off the early running. I jostle for position in a tight pack of flying elbows and take a spike in the shin.

We split the quarter in a pedestrian fifty-seven. But it might as well be five seconds faster. At least, that's how quick it feels.

With 250 to go I move up and tuck in behind Lawlor.

He puts the hammer down, and I follow him. But there's no juice in the caboose, and I hit a wall over the final one hundred.

I end up crawling home in fourth place, and medics help me to a tent to be rehydrated.

It takes half an hour before the finalists are finally posted. I squeak in as the last qualifier. Hardly the sort of result I want.

I've worked myself into quite a state by the time I climb into bed. It's useless. The heat took too much out of me.

I'm not healthy enough to break 1.50, and that's what it'll probably take to finish in the top three.

I stare at the stucco ceiling and cough up scads of mucus into toilet paper.

Sam isn't concerned, though. He snores away in the other bed.

I've got to get out of here.

I dress, catch a cab to the stadium, then clamber over a locked gate and steal my way to the wooden bleachers.

It's dead calm. Moonlight illuminates white lanes on the rubberized red track, and the smell of grass from the infield perfumes the atmosphere.

I reach into my knapsack and remove Koech's army boots. The soles are embedded with pebbles, and the leather is scuffed. I loosen the laces and run my fingers over the numbers I've written on the tongues.

1.46.3.

It ain't happening. Not this season. The illness has just taken too much of a toll.

I slip the boots onto my feet and lace up, my toes pinched by the tissue paper with which I've padded them.

It takes several minutes before I clunk down a flight of steps towards the curved start line. The collision of rubber heels on wood echoes throughout the empty stadium.

When I begin to jog, the hard track surface squeaks beneath me.

I stare at Koech. "Kulvinder brought the gun."

He lifts up my chin. "You were still in the middle of it all."

"Leave me alone."

"Don't kid yourself, Leeds."

He isn't listening. "Leave me alone."

He pulls me towards him, then tickles my underarms.

"Stop." It hurts. "Stop!"

I make a break for the bathroom and lock the door.

I don't care what Koech says; it isn't my fault.

After that, Koech spends more and more of his time at the slum. He starts a drive to collect second-hand clothes at school, and he goes to political meetings at the university. Mum and Dad argue about him getting in over his head, while I stay out of everyone's way.

I round the first bend and pick up the pace on the straight-away.

Up ahead, in lane one, is a hurdle still set up after a race earlier in the day. I gather myself and leap. There's no spring in my step; my boot tags wood and I tumble onto the track.

I lie on my back, stare up at white moon, and cough.

In the morning I warm up alone, stretching in the infield after finishing an easy set of drills.

Nearby, Kulvinder laces on his spikes.

I interrupt him. "Kulvinder."

"What d'you want?"

"Neither one of us is to blame."

He fiddles with the protruding tongue on his spikes. "Whatever."

I look him dead in the eye and clench a fist. "I mean it."

"Can we discuss this later?" He stands up.

"Wait." I grab his sleeve. "I'm not going to be able to finish the race."

"Don't be an asshole. Of course you are."

"Just shut up for a moment, okay? Last night I told myself that if I didn't feel I had a shot after warming up, I'd pace you through the first six."

"Fuck that. I don't need . . ."

"Please don't make this harder than it already is." I want to cry, and I grip onto Vivian's crucifix, which hangs around my neck. "I can suck it up enough to get you through the quarter in fifty. It'll take the sting out of the others and give you a shot at stealing the race." He stares at me. "I'll step off the track at 600. The rest is up to you."

I trot off before I can change my mind.

Erica's race gets underway first.

She's in tough with several women from Ontario. But she follows Sam's plan to the letter and leads through the first quarter.

The field is still tightly bunched at 400 despite a split of fifty-eight.

A black Nova Scotian applies pressure on the backstretch and forces Erica to make a burst that strings out the pack.

She leads by a good five metres with one hundred to go, falters slightly over the final sixty but holds the others off.

She's run 1.59.48, qualified for Tokyo and broken two minutes for the first time.

We're up next, and I'm jinking like a crack-head.

The race is being taped by CBC and is slated for broadcast a week later.

"On your mark."

BANG.

I jump out fast but still manage to settle smoothly into a rhythm by the time I reach the stagger.

I check over my shoulder; Kulvinder's right behind me.

We pass through the first 200 in twenty-three seconds. Perfect.

My legs are holding together, and I concentrate on the approaching bell lap.

I'm tempted to look back to get a sense of where the others are. But it's a waste of energy. So I just glide forward.

"47, 48, 49, 50."

Forty-nine point.

My legs start to burn, but I'm committed to taking it through the first six.

Don't think. Just go.

I can feel Kulvinder tucked in at my shoulder, and I focus on pointing my hips where I want my feet to go.

Crunch the next two.

I throw in a spurt with 300 to go, then look back when I hit the middle of the backstretch. Kulvinder and I are at least fifteen metres up on the field.

Hang in there, at least for the next one hundred.

I kick my butt with my heel and stretch forward with the other foot, lengthening my stride and staying ahead of Kulvinder.

"1.14, 1.15, 1.16, 1.17."

I move into lane two, and Kulvinder creeps past on the inside.

"C'mon Leeds," he mutters. "Just two to go."

I'm spent. But I've practised this hundreds of times. Relax the shoulders, lean into the curve, shorten my stride and build momentum going into the bend.

150 left. This is it. Flick. Surge. Flick. Flick. Flick. Stay up on your toes. Drive from the ankle. Flick.

With eighty metres to go two bodies inch by on my outside. I'm running on empty.

Pour soi, I think. *Pour soi*.

The finish bobs into view, and I focus on a spot five metres after the line. Flick. Flick.

At twenty metres I've slipped to sixth.

I can feel the balls of my feet rubbing against the soles of my spikes. There's a huge rooooar. Ten metres. Flick. Another runner rushes past.

When I cross the finish line, my chest is smouldering.

I fall against Kulvinder, and we lean against one another.

"Did . . . you . . ." I ask.

"1.47.91." He's made the team. "You're a bastard, you know."

"You're . . . welcome."

Someone taps me on the shoulder. It's Sam.

He hugs me for a long time.

"I had you at 1.49.96," he says. "A p.b."

Sam holds a team meeting before the awards banquet, and I'm lying in bed.

We hold hands and say a prayer.

He gives thanks to God, Kioko, the athletes, the guy with the starting gun, the volunteers who made the meet possible, and so on.

When he's done, Kulvinder is quick to move on.

"Are you coming to the after-party, Leeds?" His arm is planted around his fiancée's waist.

"I'm not up to it." I've puked twice in the last hour, and I'm dizzy.

"It won't be the same without you," Erica says.

"Come," Sam adds. "You've got just as much to celebrate as anyone else in the room."

Bullshit. The three of them are going to Quebec City in the morning. Kulvinder and Erica will run another eight before joining the National Team in Toronto. There they'll get outfitted in spunky red Canadian uniforms, huge maple leaves on the backs, and handed tickets to a warm-up meet in Stuttgart.

Meanwhile I'll be cutting my lawn in Vancouver.

"Don't be so hard on yourself," Sam continues. "There's always next year. Jipcho had his moment at the Commonwealth Games after sacrificing himself for Keino in Mexico City."

"Come on." Kulvinder winks. "Party with us."

I think of my last workout with Koech. During the stretch drive he grinned before accelerating for home, his steady stride leaving behind a confusion of rising dust.

When the dust finally settled, I couldn't distinguish his footprints from mine.

I smile. "Hell, why the fuck not?"

GLOSSARY

Acknowledgements

I'm grateful to the British Columbia Arts Council and the Canada Council for helping me steal time away to write. Special thanks also to George Elliot Clarke, John Edgar Wideman, Sue Sinclair and Noy Holland for their insight. Also considered thanks to Jay Neugeboren for his steadfast belief, guidance and encouragement; my editor, Barbara Berson, for her faith, her uncanny instincts and her uncompromising sense of excellence; my agent, Tom Wallace, for being a source of support; and Mr. and Mrs. Baxter for their unflagging loyalty.